DEADLY UNDERTOW

LANTERN BEACH MYSTERIES, BOOK 6

CHRISTY BARRITT

COMPLETE BOOK LIST

Squeaky Clean Mysteries:
- #1 Hazardous Duty
- #2 Suspicious Minds
- #2.5 It Came Upon a Midnight Crime (novella)
- #3 Organized Grime
- #4 Dirty Deeds
- #5 The Scum of All Fears
- #6 To Love, Honor and Perish
- #7 Mucky Streak
- #8 Foul Play
- #9 Broom & Gloom
- #10 Dust and Obey
- #11 Thrill Squeaker
- #11.5 Swept Away (novella)
- #12 Cunning Attractions
- #13 Cold Case: Clean Getaway
- #14 Cold Case: Clean Sweep
- #15 Cold Case: Clean Break

#16 Cleans to an End

While You Were Sweeping, A Riley Thomas Spinoff

The Sierra Files:
#1 Pounced

#2 Hunted

#3 Pranced

#4 Rattled

The Gabby St. Claire Diaries (a Tween Mystery series):
#1 The Curtain Call Caper

#2 The Disappearing Dog Dilemma

#3 The Bungled Bike Burglaries

The Worst Detective Ever
#1 Ready to Fumble

#2 Reign of Error

#3 Safety in Blunders

#4 Join the Flub

#5 Blooper Freak

#6 Flaw Abiding Citizen

#7 Gaffe Out Loud

#8 Joke and Dagger

#9 Wreck the Halls

#10 Glitch and Famous

#11 Not on My Botch

Raven Remington
Relentless

Holly Anna Paladin Mysteries:

#1 Random Acts of Murder

#2 Random Acts of Deceit

#2.5 Random Acts of Scrooge

#3 Random Acts of Malice

#4 Random Acts of Greed

#5 Random Acts of Fraud

#6 Random Acts of Outrage

#7 Random Acts of Iniquity

Lantern Beach Mysteries

#1 Hidden Currents

#2 Flood Watch

#3 Storm Surge

#4 Dangerous Waters

#5 Perilous Riptide

#6 Deadly Undertow

Lantern Beach Romantic Suspense

#1 Tides of Deception

#2 Shadow of Intrigue

#3 Storm of Doubt

#4 Winds of Danger

#5 Rains of Remorse

#6 Torrents of Fear

Lantern Beach P.D.

#1 On the Lookout

#2 Attempt to Locate

#3 First Degree Murder

#4 Dead on Arrival

#5 Plan of Action

Lantern Beach Escape

Afterglow (a novelette)

Lantern Beach Blackout

#1 Dark Water

#2 Safe Harbor

#3 Ripple Effect

#4 Rising Tide

Lantern Beach Guardians

#1 Hide and Seek

#2 Shock and Awe

#3 Safe and Sound

Lantern Beach Blackout: The New Recruits

#1 Rocco

#2 Axel

#3 Beckett

#4 Gabe

Lantern Beach Mayday

#1 Run Aground

#2 Dead Reckoning

#3 Tipping Point

Lantern Beach Blackout: Danger Rising

#1 Brandon

#2 Dylan

#3 Maddox

#4 Titus

Lantern Beach Christmas

Silent Night

Crime á la Mode

#1 Dead Man's Float

#2 Milkshake Up

#3 Bomb Pop Threat

#4 Banana Split Personalities

Beach Bound Books and Beans Mysteries

#1 Bound by Murder

#2 Bound by Disaster

#3 Bound by Mystery

#4 Bound by Trouble

#5 Bound by Mayhem

Vanishing Ranch

#1 Forgotten Secrets

#2 Necessary Risk

#3 Risky Ambition

#4 Deadly Intent

#5 Lethal Betrayal

#6 High Stakes Deception

#7 Fatal Vendetta

#8 Troubled Tidings

#9 Narrow Escape

The Sidekick's Survival Guide

#1 The Art of Eavesdropping

#2 The Perks of Meddling

#3 The Exercise of Interfering

#4 The Practice of Prying

#5 The Skill of Snooping

#6 The Craft of Being Covert

Saltwater Cowboys

#1 Saltwater Cowboy

#2 Breakwater Protector

#3 Cape Corral Keeper

#4 Seagrass Secrets

#5 Driftwood Danger

#6 Unwavering Security

Beach House Mysteries

#1 The Cottage on Ghost Lane

#2 The Inn on Hanging Hill

#3 The House on Dagger Point

School of Hard Rocks Mysteries

#1 The Treble with Murder

#2 Crime Strikes a Chord

#3 Tone Death

Carolina Moon Series

#1 Home Before Dark

#2 Gone By Dark

#3 Wait Until Dark

#4 Light the Dark

#5 Taken By Dark

Suburban Sleuth Mysteries:

Death of the Couch Potato's Wife

Fog Lake Suspense:

#1 Edge of Peril

#2 Margin of Error

#3 Brink of Danger

#4 Line of Duty

#5 Legacy of Lies

#6 Secrets of Shame

#7 Refuge of Redemption

Cape Thomas Series:

#1 Dubiosity

#2 Disillusioned

#3 Distorted

Standalone Romantic Mystery:

The Good Girl

Suspense:

Imperfect

The Wrecking

Sweet Christmas Novella:

Home to Chestnut Grove

Standalone Romantic-Suspense:

Keeping Guard

The Last Target

Race Against Time

Ricochet

Key Witness

Lifeline

High-Stakes Holiday Reunion

Desperate Measures

Hidden Agenda

Mountain Hideaway

Dark Harbor

Shadow of Suspicion

The Baby Assignment

The Cradle Conspiracy

Trained to Defend

Mountain Survival

Dangerous Mountain Rescue

Nonfiction:

Characters in the Kitchen

Changed: True Stories of Finding God through Christian Music (out of print)

The Novel in Me: The Beginner's Guide to Writing and Publishing a Novel (out of print)

PROLOGUE
23 WEEKS EARLIER

CADY MATTHEWS LISTENED to the dull sound of her boots hitting the cement beneath her. She tried to pace her steps instead of listening to her instincts and breaking out into a run.

The sun was setting, but that wasn't what made the area around her seem gray. Nor was it the tall buildings blocking the sunlight that made the sky constantly dismal. The truth was, darkness had simply descended onto the God-forsaken area.

Cady did know one thing. She wanted to leave.

Now.

And she didn't need anyone's approval.

Cady had slipped away from the gang's compound —an old apartment complex in a shady part of downtown Seattle—to go to work at the drugstore, just as she did every evening.

Except tonight, she wouldn't.

She glanced over her shoulder, feeling like she was being watched.

She saw no one. Not yet.

Cady was going to walk away from this assignment, turn in all the evidence she'd collected, and do her best to resume her life.

Somehow.

She wasn't sure what that life would look like now.

But maybe she and Ryan could plan their future. Maybe they could get married, move somewhere quiet and peaceful, and nail down the things that were really important in life.

It wasn't about money or power or titles.

It was about people. Love. Family.

Even as the thought crossed Cady's mind, she knew reality didn't match up with her dreams. Ryan was career-driven. If he had to choose between Cady and his job as a prosecuting attorney for the county, she'd be on the side of the road, a barely visible image in Ryan's rearview mirror.

Her stomach clenched at the thought. Not being your fiancé's top priority was hard to swallow. But she should be used to it. When had she ever been anyone's top priority?

Never.

Not even her parents.

She'd deal with those thoughts later.

Right now, Cady had to focus on staying alive.

She hiked her fake leather purse higher on her shoulder and hurried down the cracked sidewalk, kicking a used syringe out of the way. No one wanted to venture into this part of town—not if they wanted to keep their lives and well-being.

But, against all odds, Cady had managed to blend in. She was a rich white girl—her parents were one of the wealthiest couples in the country. She'd grown up with every privilege imaginable.

Yet she'd somehow adapted to this assignment, going undercover as a street-smart gang member.

Perhaps it was perseverance that had gotten her this far. Ambition. The fact that she'd hardly failed at anything.

Then again, maybe that was all working to her detriment. If she hadn't grown up with that can-do attitude, maybe she would have said no when she'd been approached about going undercover in one of the country's most dangerous gangs, DH-7.

Just ahead, on the corner, she spotted the drugstore where she worked. The location also served as a place to exchange communication with her contact on the task force.

Her spine stiffened as she started to cross the intersection, and she looked over her shoulder again. She saw no one unusual. A man loitered outside the door to his apartment building. A boy bounced a basketball, no doubt headed to the quarters two blocks away. A woman—most likely a prostitute—paced a four-foot section of cement across the street while smoking a cigarette.

Cady's gut told her someone was watching her.

A member of DH-7?

Since they suspected a traitor in their midst, it was a good possibility.

She needed to go inside the drugstore. Work for a little while, just like normal. Especially if she was being watched.

And then, a little later, she could slip away out the back door.

Call a cab?

No, that was too risky.

Call for backup?

There probably wasn't time.

She wasn't sure yet. This hadn't been her exit plan, so she was going to have to wing it.

As soon as she had clocked in, donned an ugly blue smock, and taken her place behind the front register, a familiar face walked in.

Bill. A patrol officer. A contact whom she could feed information.

He laid a pack of gum and a bottle of Coke on the counter. His eyes showed only a hint of recognition as Cady rang him. To anyone watching, they were strangers.

"I heard a storm is brewing out in the Pacific." He nodded behind her at the long, narrow window in the front of the store. "A big one."

Cady's breath caught at his underlying message. "Is that right?"

"Forecasters are saying it's going to be bad."

"What are they telling people to do?" Her hands trembled as she put the gum and soda in a bag.

"People in its path need to evacuate. All the models they set up have proven themselves inaccurate. Like always. They say to never believe a weatherman."

Her heart thumped in her chest as she chewed on his coded words. Trouble was coming—and it wasn't going to be good. The models that had been set up? That meant the plan they'd set in place for this assignment. Something had gone wrong.

What could that be?

Cady needed to flee. And the sooner the better.

She handed the officer his bag and smiled. "Have a good evening."

He gave her one last warning glance.

She got his message loud and clear—there was no time to waste.

As soon as he was out the door, Cady slipped from behind the counter. She needed to go to the back of the store and escape. Now.

"Cady, where you going?" Mr. Jenkins, her boss, stepped from the beauty aisle where he'd been restocking lipstick and stared at her.

"I need a bathroom break."

"You just got here."

"Female problems." No one ever argued with that—especially not men.

He sighed long and hard. "Don't take too long. I need someone to man the register. Anita already called in sick."

"Got it."

He paused before muttering, "Good help is hard to find."

She mentally sent an apology. Yes, good help was hard to find. And poor Mr. Jenkins always seemed to be at his wit's end. He'd obviously drawn the short straw when he'd been assigned to this location.

Cady's hands shook as she rushed past the aisle filled with stomach and indigestion aids.

The "Employees Only" sign at the back of the store was now within sight. She just had to go through that door, grab her purse, and then she'd run. Fast and furious. As hard as she could.

And she wouldn't look back.

Ever.

Just as her hands hit the door—just as she felt freedom within her grasp—someone called her name.

All the blood drained from her face as she paused. She knew that voice. She squeezed her eyes shut, wishing this was just a nightmare.

Cady knew it wasn't.

Slowly, she composed herself and turned.

Orion, Raul's right-hand man, stood there glaring at her. His light brown skin glistened with sweat, and his black hair was pulled back into a tight ponytail. His eyes held the cold, hard look of someone who would rip another person from limb to limb if that's what it took to advance his agenda.

And it was even worse when he was high.

Which he was right now. His pupils were dilated,

his motions faster than usual, and his chest rose and fell too quickly.

She glanced around, making sure Mr. Jenkins wasn't nearby, and lowered her voice. "What are you doing here?"

Orion stared at her, the wicked look in his eyes causing her to shudder. He had no respect for life. No respect for anyone or anything but himself and his own agenda.

"Raul sent me to get you. Me and Tyron."

Cady looked over as another man joined them, someone she'd only seen from a distance. A twenty-something man, on the short side, but thick with sinewy muscles.

She didn't have time to observe him for too long because Orion's words echoed in her mind.

"Raul sent you to get me?" She could hardly breathe.

Was this it? Was this the moment she died? Where it all ended?

"Something happened," Orion said. "He wants to talk to you about it."

"Just me?" This couldn't be good.

Orion shrugged, his upper lip twitching like he had a bad taste in his mouth. "I dunno. Maybe every-one. I just know I have to get you. No questions asked."

"Better be important. Might cost me my job."

Orion narrowed his eyes and let out a cool breath. "You know you don't need this job."

Tyron stood in the background, as if he was just here to be the muscles, the one who stood lookout.

Cady leaned closer to Orion and lowered her voice. "I've been getting you guys drugs so you can make meth. It's working out in all of our favor."

Cady had actually paid for the drugs, unable to bring herself to steal them.

"That's small potatoes compared to what we're doing. You know that. Now come on." He grabbed her arm. Tight. Too tight.

She wanted to argue. To refuse. But if she did, she'd only be setting herself up for failure. She had no choice but to go with Orion and Tyron. She slipped her smock off and dropped it on the floor.

But as she left with the men, Cady's life flashed before her eyes with every beat of her heart . . . beats that might soon be nonexistent.

CHAPTER
ONE

CASSIDY STEPPED BACK from the dining room table and smiled at what she saw.

"What do you think, Kujo?" She looked down at the golden retriever sitting beside her, his tongue hanging toward the floor like a banner proclaiming happiness.

He let out a quick but enthusiastic bark.

"You approve?" she confirmed. "You think Ty will like it?"

The dog barked again.

Cassidy patted his head, his soft fur feeling luxurious against her fingertips. "I know I can always count on you, boy."

Was this what her life had boiled down to over the past week? Talking to Ty's dog like it was a normal thing? Was she that desperate for Ty to return?

He'd been gone for seven days, visiting his mother who was having surgery. Her ovarian cancer had spread, and doctors had no choice but to operate since chemo and radiation hadn't worked. Thankfully, the surgery had gone well, and Del was now at home recovering.

Cassidy wished she could have gone with Ty. But she couldn't leave Lantern Beach—not without serious risk of blowing everything. Since the trial against members of DH-7 was only a month away, she needed to sit tight and bide her time until she could mark this chapter of her life closed.

Strangely enough, being in hiding was one of the best things that could have happened to her.

In thirty minutes, when Ty pulled into his driveway—provided he was on time—Cassidy was going to surprise him with brunch. She'd made a fruit salad, blueberry muffins, and a spinach and sausage quiche.

Just for fun, Cassidy had added a white tablecloth to cover the jaundiced wood of the old seventies-style dining room table. She'd topped the linen with some candles and the finest dishes she could find at her rental —which just happened to be old with brown flowers on the edges. The September day was beautiful—in the mid-seventies—so she'd opened her windows, and a pleasant breeze made the whole house aflutter with excitement.

In all of its imperfections, the setup still seemed simply perfect.

Outside, the sound of tires crunching against the gravel drive leading to her beach cottage caught her ear.

Ty.

Her heart surged. He was early. And Cassidy was more than okay with that.

Quickly, she ran a hand through her long blonde hair and straightened her blousy shirt.

Cassidy hadn't expected to miss Ty this much. After all, she'd always been the independent type. But Ty had gained an unmistakable place in her heart over the past few months—a place she wanted to keep him forever and always.

Kujo barked, obviously hearing the vehicle and anticipating the arrival of his owner as well.

"We both missed him, didn't we?" she murmured.

Kujo barked again, almost as if he understood every word she said. It was just one more reason she loved the canine.

Cassidy did one last check of the house, made sure everything was in place, and then listened as footsteps ascended the weathered, wooden stairs outside her beach cottage.

She started toward the door when she smelled something faint but unpleasant.

Smoke.

The quiche!

How could she have forgotten it was in the oven?

She hurried toward the kitchen and grabbed an oven mitt. As soon as Cassidy pulled the pan out, she scrunched her nose at the blackened mess in the pie dish. The recipe was ruined.

So much for the romantic breakfast she'd planned as a welcome home.

Cassidy frowned and tried to think of a quick solution.

Before she could, a knock sounded at the door. Hopefully the open windows would air the smoke from the place quickly. Otherwise, her surprise meal would be a surprise trip to the clinic for a breathing treatment.

Thankfully, Ty was the forgiving type.

Cassidy set the charred quiche in the sink and tossed a towel over it. Then she hurried across the room and threw the front door open, figuring she'd make the best of things.

But it wasn't Ty standing on the other side.

Her stomach dropped more quickly than an anchor during a squall.

It was . . . "Ryan?"

A grin lit Ryan Samson's perfectly chiseled face—a face she hadn't seen in months. Without invitation, he stepped inside with outstretched arms.

"Cad—Cassidy!" His voice rolled over her, as smooth and polished as he was. "I've missed you. And you look great. Beach life really agrees with you."

Before she realized what was happening, Ryan embraced her. His familiar scent—a spicy blend that always reminded her of the smell of money—filled her senses and took her back in time. Back to her old life. Back to the person she used to be before DH-7 had turned her life upside down.

Cassidy stiffened, her thoughts clashing inside her. She couldn't make sense of them right now, so instead she stepped back and looked at Ryan.

Ryan . . .

He was here. In Lantern Beach. After not speaking to Cassidy for nearly four months.

He hadn't changed much in the time since Cassidy had seen him last. Even though he was in a beach town, he wore a designer gray pullover and dress slacks that probably cost as much as one week's rent at some of the smaller beach cottages in the area.

He still had dark brown hair that was styled with perfection—despite the area's wind and humidity. He was clean-shaven, picture perfect, and screamed of someone with a future in politics. The camera loved him. People loved him. And he had a great record for putting away the bad guys.

Kujo sat beside Cassidy, a low growl rumbling in his chest. She patted the canine's head, trying to quietly assure him that everything was okay—okay being a relative term right now.

Cassidy stepped away from Ryan's embrace and shook her head in disbelief. "What are you doing here? I'm . . . shocked to say the least."

"What? I thought you'd be happy to see me." He shrugged, looking equal parts arrogantly offended and coolly unaffected. He'd always been the aloof type, the king of logic and level-headedness.

So much so that he'd persuaded Cassidy to keep their relationship a secret back when they'd been together in Seattle. At the time, Cassidy had convinced herself it made sense. Now . . . it just felt slimy and wrong.

"Kujo, it's okay," she murmured, trying to get the dog to stop growling before someone got hurt—that someone being Ryan.

The canine gave one last grumble before stopping to give Ryan a death stare instead.

Where did Cassidy even start this conversation? She closed the door and turned toward her ex, a sense of dread seizing her. What would have led him to find her? Whatever it was, it couldn't be good.

"How'd you find me?" She looked out the window for any signs of trouble. "Did anyone follow you here?"

Ryan let out a puff of air, combined with a deprecating chuckle. "I'll explain everything. Give me time. And of course no one followed me. I'm not stupid."

Cassidy crossed her arms, still on edge. Ryan showing up here was not normal. Or expected. Or okay.

Nor was his superior attitude.

"Why are you here? Did something happen? Didn't you get my messages?" The questions rushed out, all equally important and pressing and impossible to prioritize.

"We have a lot to talk about. I thought it was best if I came here so we could figure this out face-to-face." In one motion, he pulled Cassidy into his arms again. He stroked her back and murmured into her hair, "It's so good to see you, to hold you. I've missed you so much."

As Cassidy stiffened and tried to push away, she heard a footstep. She craned her neck to see beyond Ryan, and her fears were realized.

Ty stood at the open door—a total contrast to Ryan

in his faded jeans and flannel shirt. Ty's hair was messy, his jaw unshaven, and his eyes warm.

Picture perfect? Maybe not if you were a politician. But Ty embodied everything that Cassidy found appealing—he exuded a manliness that polished Ryan would never reach.

Kujo ran to greet him, the dog's welcome much warmer now.

The shocked and then hardened expression on Ty's face said it all. This was not the welcome he'd envisioned.

Cassidy stepped back, a rush of nerves rising in her. She liked to keep a cool head, but this was just uncomfortable . . . and unfortunate. And horrible, horrible timing all around.

She turned toward Ty, and Ryan followed her gaze. Ty's hands were on his hips, and the air crackled with awkwardness all around them.

"Ty!" She wanted to rush into his arms, but until she and Ryan talked more, that also felt awkward. Instead, Cassidy stepped forward and grabbed his arm, pulling him closer before whispering, "I'll explain all of this."

Ty's gaze went from Cassidy to Ryan and then back to Cassidy. Her words apparently didn't reassure him, and he put on what Cassidy called his "SEAL about to jump into action" face.

"What's going on?" Ty's words sounded a lot like Kujo's rumbling growl.

Ryan stepped forward, his hand outstretched like any good elected official determined to win over the favor of the masses. "I'm Ryan Samson. Pleasure to meet you."

Ty stared at his hand but didn't return the gesture. His perceptive eyes continued to study the situation. "Ty Chambers."

Ryan coolly assessed Ty.

Two alphas in one room? There was no way this would turn out well.

"Ty, I'm going to need some time alone with Cad—Cassidy." Ryan said the words like he expected everyone to listen—which was what generally happened in his life.

But not here on Lantern Beach.

Ryan was *not* going to step back into Cassidy's life and begin to dictate what she did and didn't do—or who came and went, for that matter.

"That's not necessary." Cassidy still held to Ty's arm. "I'd prefer that Ty be here."

Ryan narrowed his eyes as if the idea was preposterous. "Unless he's got clearance, you know the details we need to discuss are confidential."

She wanted to argue with Ryan, but she knew his words were true. What the two of them needed to talk about wasn't light or casual conversation. The details were all classified, and Cassidy had even signed a form to ensure it. In this case, she'd have to put her own desires and wishes on the back burner, like it or not.

Or not being her choice.

"Okay," Cassidy said. "I get it. But first I need to talk to Ty. Alone. Outside."

Tension built in Cassidy's chest with every second the three of them were in the same room.

Ty drew his gaze away from Ryan, his features as stony and hard as a soldier on the battlefield making the call to fight or retreat. "Of course."

Cassidy led him to the deck, away from the window, so Ryan couldn't overhear anything. As soon as she stepped outside, the sound of waves rolling in the Atlantic Ocean filled her senses. The sun hit her face. A family played Frisbee on the beach nearby.

This was her happy place.

Normally.

Right now, tension gripped her in a chokehold that made it hard to breathe.

As soon as they were far enough away, she grabbed Ty's arms, knowing she didn't have much time to get through to him, to say what she needed to say.

"Is that your ex-fiancé?" Ty started.

"Yes. I had no idea Ryan was going to come here. He literally showed up on my doorstep two minutes before you arrived."

Ty studied her gaze, his perceptive eyes absorbing everything. "Does he know you're not engaged anymore?"

"I don't know. I'd . . . planned a breakfast for you. That's what the smoke was from . . . but that's a different story. I wanted to hear about your mom. And . . . I've missed you terribly."

Cassidy wanted to embrace him. Kiss him. Enjoy their time together.

Ty dipped his head, his eyes softening. "I've missed you too. I want to be there to hear whatever he has to say. I already know what's going on."

Her gut twisted. "But you're not supposed to know. And Ryan can't speak about the details in front of people who aren't approved. He's a by-the-rules kind of guy. You know what that's like from your days as a SEAL. It's out of my control."

She silently begged him to understand.

Ty pressed his lips together, his gaze simmering, and tension causing his jaw muscles to jump. "So I'm just supposed to go home?"

"Just for a few minutes. I'm sure Ryan won't be here long. I . . . I just don't know what's going on. He wouldn't have come unless it was important. I do know that."

Ty let out a long puff of air. He considered himself her protector—and he wouldn't let the law stand in the way of that. Yet he also respected her.

"Cassidy . . ."

She squeezed his arms again. "I know. I do. Believe me. Just let me talk to Ryan, okay? And I'm sorry. I didn't want it to be like this."

Ty glanced back at the door one last time. "You're a smart woman. I'll trust your judgment and respect your choice."

Cassidy kissed his cheek, relieved that he understood. "Thank you. I'll be over as soon as I can."

Ty nodded, but his neck looked stiff and his eyes

hard. "Kujo can stay with you to make sure your 'friend' doesn't misbehave."

Cassidy turned back to the house, unsure if she was excited to hear an update from Ryan or if she should dread it. Maybe for now she would just settle on getting this over with.

CHAPTER
TWO

CASSIDY CLOSED the door behind her and soaked in Ryan once more. He hadn't changed much since she'd last seen him. He was still professional and confident—some might say arrogant. Still handsome and well put together—maybe even stuck-up. Still driven in a way that had impressed her family—and that should have been her first warning sign to run.

At one time, he'd seemed to be the perfect fit for her life.

Until Cassidy had realized he wasn't. Not even close.

He stood by her couch, absently flipping through a Day-at-a-Glance calendar on her end table. He set it down when Cassidy and Kujo came back inside. A smile brushed his lips but quickly disappeared. Perhaps he'd finally realized how awkward his sudden appearance had made her life.

But Cassidy also knew if Ryan was here, there was a reason. An update. A motive.

He wasn't the type to break protocol at a whim.

"I know you wonder what I'm doing here." He shoved his hands into his pockets.

She licked her lips, all the moisture gone from her mouth. "I texted. Did you not get my messages? I haven't heard from you in months. And now you're here. And . . ." Where did Cassidy even start?

"I lost that phone." A knot formed between his eyebrows. "Didn't Samuel give you the message?"

"Samuel knew?" Samuel Stephens was the task force leader, an FBI agent, and Cassidy's contact from her detective job in Seattle.

And Ryan had lost his phone? Did that mean he'd never gotten that text where she broke up with him? Cassidy had tried to call multiple times, but Ryan hadn't answered. She'd figured it was because he was too busy flirting with his new assistant. Cassidy had seen enough of their pictures together online to know the truth.

"Of course Samuel knew. But that's the other thing I need to tell you." Ryan squinted, and his jaw flexed, just like it always did when he tried to find the right words. "Maybe we should sit down."

"Maybe we should." Cassidy's head swirled with so many thoughts and questions. It would take a while to sort all of this out. There was just so much to talk about, so much information to cover.

Cassidy sat on one end of the couch, and Ryan sat

near her—too near. He reached for her hand and squeezed it.

She pulled away, knowing without a doubt she needed to set some boundaries and fast.

Cassidy had too much to lose here—namely, Ty. Instead, she set her hand in her lap, a new swell of emotion battering her when she saw the hurt and confusion in Ryan's gaze.

"Ryan . . . I tried to call. I sent messages. I . . . I don't know how to say this, so I'm just going to put it out there. I broke things off between us."

"You what?" His eyes widened, and his voice stretched thin with shock.

"I did. I'm . . . I'm sorry. I thought you knew."

"I didn't."

She remembered those pictures of him and his new assistant, and her compassion waned.

"My love life isn't really what I want to talk about right now." Although, Cassidy did want answers. Love —or lack thereof—wasn't what had brought him here. "I need to know what's going on with the case. Why you would risk coming here. What's going on with Samuel."

Ryan's expression didn't look nearly as warm as he straightened, carefully tugging at his sleeves and morphing back into his aloof, professional demeanor. "Of course. I should start from the beginning."

Kujo sat on the floor between Ryan and Cassidy, on guard. Cassidy stroked the dog's head, grateful for the distraction. Her insides felt like they were being ripped in two with the tension, and she dreaded wherever this conversation might go. She instinctively knew her life was hanging in the balance here.

Ryan locked gazes with her, his stormy expression dead serious. "Now it's my turn to give you uncomfortable news. I don't know how to tell you this, but we believe Samuel was working for DH-7."

"What?" Cassidy blinked, unable to believe her ears. "No . . ."

Samuel was her friend. Her confidante. He would never betray her. Would never work for the very people they were fighting against.

"I'm sorry," Ryan said. "I know you trusted him. But that's what all the evidence points to."

"He wouldn't do that." Cassidy swung her head back and forth with enough force that the room started to rock. She wouldn't believe it. Couldn't. Refused.

"None of us want to think it's true," Ryan said. "But he came into the office, stole all the evidence against DH-7, and took off. No one has heard from him since. We've suspected from the start that there was someone on the inside working with the gang. Now we know."

Cassidy recalled some of her last conversations with Samuel. "Samuel said you had another inside man wrapped up in DH-7. He made it sound like someone you'd hired."

Ryan's headshake was so subtle she thought she'd imagined it. But she could also see anger simmer beneath the coiled action.

"Samuel lied," Ryan said. "*He* was the one on the

inside, and it wasn't because we asked him to be there. He double-crossed us. All of us. Me. You. The system."

Cassidy squeezed the skin between her eyes, trying to comprehend everything Ryan was telling her. "If that's true, why didn't Samuel come here to kill me? He would want me dead. I'm the biggest threat to the whole gang. I'm the one who's going to bring them down."

Ryan shifted, pressed his lips together, and sighed. "That's the other thing, Cad—Cassidy. I'll get your new name right one day. We're afraid that just might be the case. It's one of the reasons I came here to find you. We fear Samuel does want you dead."

It felt like a sweeping frost spread over her body. Her heart.

Betrayal by the bad guys? That was expected. Betrayal by someone you considered a friend? It was gut-wrenching.

"But . . . you didn't even know where I was, Ryan. Only Samuel did." It just didn't add up. None of this did.

"Your parents hired a private investigator." Ryan slowed the cadence of his words like Cassidy might need time to comprehend them.

"I heard. But they called him off."

Ryan remained silent a minute, studying Cassidy with his gaze. "Why did you think that?"

"Because Samuel told me—" Cassidy stopped herself. If Samuel was in on this, then she couldn't trust anything the man had told her—and that fact would change everything.

"No, your parents didn't call him off," he said. "The PI—Ricky Ernest—actually came to me last week. He found a video online that some tourists here in Lantern Beach captured on their cell phone camera. Three men had apparently taken flakka and were on a rampage on the boardwalk. As expected, they looked and acted like zombies. I believe you stepped in to help."

Cassidy closed her eyes. Yes, she *had* done that. And, yes, people *had* filmed it. She'd hoped it wouldn't go viral and wouldn't lead to her discovery. But the footage had, and there was nothing she could do about it now.

"So that brought you to Lantern Beach?" She was still trying to let all of this sink in. It would take a while. The problem was, Cassidy didn't have a while. "Even if all that is true, that doesn't explain why you're here."

Ryan coming here could blow Cassidy's cover, thrust her in danger, and put her testimony at risk. It wasn't a smart move, despite everything that had happened. But Ryan was never impulsive. She needed to hear him out.

"I did some research," Ryan said. "Even though your face was never directly in any news articles here, I read enough to learn your true identity. And if I could do that, so could members of DH-7."

"What are you saying, Ryan?" Cassidy knew exactly what he was saying. But she needed to hear the words

—the bottom line—herself. Needed time for the truth to sink in.

Ryan's gaze locked on hers as he prepared to drive home his point just like any good lawyer would. "I'm saying you need to leave. It's almost time for the trial, and we need your testimony. You're not safe here."

"I'm not leaving Lantern Beach."

His gaze narrowed, and irritation inched over his features. "You would put everything in jeopardy just to stay here?"

"I don't want to put anything in jeopardy. But I'm tired of running."

He sighed, rubbed a hand over his face, and leaned back. "You're in love with that man, aren't you? Ty?"

Cassidy shifted, feeling uncomfortable yet strangely confident and sure of herself. "I am."

Ryan looked down at his hands, as if processing his thoughts. She gave him a minute, not giving in to the urge to explain or apologize or try to justify her actions. In many ways, Ryan had dug his own hole.

"This isn't going the way I thought it would," he finally said.

That made two of them.

"I can't believe you came. You could have called." It seemed so mundane to say that after everything else they'd talked about. Yet Cassidy still had so many questions. There was so much that didn't make sense.

"I was given strict orders by Lambert—he's the one who took over for Samuel—to bring you back myself. I figured I was the best bet since your location is still supposed to be a secret."

Cassidy needed more time to think this through. What she thought she knew had been turned upside down. It would take a while for things to make sense. "Tell me more about Samuel."

Ryan leaned back again, his arm casually draped across the back of the couch. "There's not much to tell. He disappeared—along with key evidence—and no one can get in touch with him. That happened about a week ago."

A week ago . . . that was the last time Cassidy had heard from Samuel.

Could her friend really have been behind this? She didn't want to think it was true. She'd trusted Samuel. Told him information. He'd even helped Cassidy out.

In fact, she had a copy of some of that evidence that had supposedly gone missing. Samuel had risked everything to send it to her. Why would he send her classified documents if he was working for DH-7?

Cassidy wanted to offer up that tidbit of information. But she didn't.

Something internal—and unknown—stopped her. Sometimes it was better to keep things quiet, to not share every secret.

Blessed are the quiet, for in the silence wisdom grows.

It was a quote from her Day-at-a-Glance calendar and all of its never-ending wisdom. As long as Cassidy lived, she didn't think the calendar would ever stop speaking to her.

"We should go, Cassidy." Ryan stood and held out his hand. "I know that's not what you want to hear, but you need to think of the bigger picture here."

As she stared at his hand, everything inside her rebelled against taking it. Seeing him. Trusting him. "I can't leave, Ryan."

A twinge of annoyance flashed across his gaze. "You have to think of people besides yourself."

His words hit Cassidy like a slap in the face, and her body went rigid. "Thinking of other people is the entire reason I've put my entire life on hold for almost a year. So don't talk to me about putting others before myself. I gave up everything for this assignment."

"Including me, apparently."

Anger surged through Cassidy, and she started to retort. Before she could, Ryan raised his hands in surrender.

"All right, all right. I'm sorry. I should have known that wasn't the best method of getting through to you." He reached into his pocket, pulled something out, and put it on the table—a card with a phone number scribbled on it. "I figured you might be stubborn, so I got a room at the inn in town. I'll give you until tomorrow to change your mind. In the meantime, here's my information."

She stared at the paper before glancing back at Ryan again. "And if I don't change my mind?"

His gaze darkened. "You should seriously consider changing your mind."

"You mentioned that."

"We still have more things to talk about," he continued, his hands going into his pockets again. "But I'm going to give you some time to process this. Besides, I've got a bit of jet lag from travel, and I could use some rest myself. I'll be in touch later today, okay?"

Cassidy nodded, knowing it was no use to argue. Not right now. "We'll be in touch then."

"Yes, we will. We definitely will."

AS SOON AS Ryan was gone, Cassidy rushed over to Ty's house, Kujo on her heels. He met her at the door and caught Cassidy in his embrace. And it was a desperate kind of embrace, the kind where Cassidy clung to him as if her life itself depended on Ty being strong enough to hold her up.

And he was. He always was.

"What's wrong?" Ty's muscles bristled beneath her. "Did he do something?"

Cassidy glanced behind her, making sure no one was watching. Suddenly, her nerves felt shot. If Ryan had found her, anyone could. He was right.

Was there anywhere safe?

She just saw the beach. Dunes. A few tourists playing sand soccer.

"I'm not sure if we should talk here," she said. Her cottage was the most likely place someone would track her down, and Ty's place was just next door.

"Let's go somewhere else then."

Ty stepped out his door and, with a steady hand on Cassidy's back, led her downstairs. Kujo followed behind them, always the faithful companion. Once on the driveway below, they climbed into Ty's vintage Chevy truck. Kujo sat between them in the middle, taking his rightful place.

Cassidy loved how Ty didn't ask any questions. How he didn't hesitate. How he jumped in to help her like a lifeguard with only one mission: to save the drowning. And Cassidy definitely felt like she was going under, being pulled by an unseen but powerful force.

Neither said anything as they rode down the street. There would be time to talk when neither of them had any distractions. Cassidy wanted to look into Ty's eyes, to read the thoughts there as she gave him the update. Besides, the silence gave her time to process.

But before they reached their destination, blue and red lights flashed behind them.

"I'm getting pulled over?" Ty muttered. "What?"

He hadn't been speeding, and Cassidy could think of no other reason why a cop might stop them.

Ty eased onto the side of the highway. An empty lot full of marsh grass and an abandoned boat was on one side of the vehicle, and across the street were rows and rows of mostly rental houses with paths leading to the ocean.

As Ty cranked down his window, Cassidy felt for the gun in her waistband. She didn't know whom she could trust at this point. Even though some of the corruption had been culled from the island's police department, their reputation was tarnished as far as Cassidy was concerned.

Officer Brad Quinton strode up to their window and stooped his gangly self down to see them. His Adam's apple bobbed up and down as he assessed them for a moment. "Hello, Ty. Caylee."

"Cassidy," she corrected.

He ignored her. "I thought I saw you guys go past."

"What's going on?" Ty leaned out the window, the balmy September air floating inside. The breeze ruffled Kujo's hair, and he leaned his muzzle into it and sniffed.

Cassidy didn't like Quinton, but she'd learned to take the good with the bad when it came to interacting with the dim-witted officer. Earlier in the month when Ty found himself falsely accused, Quinton had both helped with the case and he'd nearly gotten Ty killed. To say her feelings were mixed would be an understatement.

Quinton's gaze traveled to Cassidy. "Someone's looking for you."

Her blood pressure surged at his blunt words. "Who would that be?"

He shrugged and glanced around, scooting closer to them as cars loaded with kayaks and fishing poles zoomed past on the highway. "I don't know. He came into the police station and showed me your picture. Except you had dark hair in the photo. Almost didn't recognize you. Still not completely certain it wasn't just someone who simply looked similar."

Ty squeezed her hand, as if he could sense Cassidy's rising panic.

"What else did he say?" Cassidy asked.

"Said you might be wanted on some charges. Gang related."

Cassidy's eyes widened as Quinton's words settled in her mind. She reached for her neck, felt the tattoo that she'd involuntarily gotten there. One that affiliated her with DH-7. She'd covered the green lightning bolt with makeup, but sometimes it reappeared at the worst times.

"That I'm wanted on gang charges?" she finally croaked out with a dry laugh. "That's ridiculous."

"What did you tell him?" Ty stole a quick glance at her, worry in his gaze.

Quinton's eyes traveled from Cassidy to Ty.

She held her breath. What *had* he said? Had Quinton settled this for her? Would his conversation with this stranger be the deciding factor in whether or not Cassidy stayed or left Lantern Beach?

Maybe.

"I asked for his law enforcement badge," Quinton finally said. "He told me he was a PI and didn't have one."

She released the air from her lungs. At least the man had asked for a badge—she hadn't felt confident Quinton would even do that. "And then you . . . ?"

"I told him I wasn't in the habit of sharing information about people who may or may not be here on the island without the proper persuasion. I mean, without the proper legal documentation." His cheeks reddened.

Cassidy turned away before Quinton saw her roll her eyes.

"What did the man say then?" Ty asked.

"That if I did see you, I should be careful. That you were dangerous." He laughed, like the very idea was crazy.

Cassidy kept her expression neutral. "What did this guy look like?"

Had it been Ryan? It didn't seem like something he would do. But who else would go to the police station on the very day Ryan arrived in town?

Unless someone had followed him.

What about Ricky Ernest, the PI her parents had hired? Cassidy used to date the man. He was more familiar with how she looked than she wanted to admit and had a better likelihood of picking her out of crowds.

Running sounded better and better all the time.

But leaving seemed like the worst thing in the world.

"He was average height," Quinton said. "Light brown hair. I think his eyes were blue. Not really sure."

Did that fit Ricky's description?

Maybe. It had been a while since Cassidy had seen him, and none of his features were particularly outstanding.

"So why did you come find us?" Ty squinted against the midmorning sun.

"I figured I owed you a favor," Quinton said. "I mean, I did almost send Ty to prison for life. I figured the least I could do was give you a heads-up."

"Did you tell Mac?" Cassidy asked.

Their friend Mac MacArthur was filling in as police chief until the town hired someone else.

"He's out and about today. There's a big fishing tournament going on down near the boardwalk, and a few of the participants have grudges against each other."

"He's trying to head off trouble?" Ty asked.

"I actually think he wants a front-row seat. He even mentioned something about bringing popcorn, but he was joking . . . I think."

In spite of everything, Cassidy smiled. That sounded like Mac.

"Anyway, I don't know who this guy is or what he wants with you or if you were a hardened criminal in your past life . . . but I'm letting you know. Just this once, I won't ask any questions."

"Thanks, Quinton." Cassidy nodded at him, honestly grateful. At least the man was attempting to redeem himself.

It looked like she had two situations to deal with right now. Handle either of them the wrong way, and Cassidy could be a dead woman.

Ty stopped just where Cassidy thought he might: the old lighthouse at the south end of the island.

There was a lot of history here—not just island history, but Cassidy and Ty's history also. The place had been both a refuge and a place of danger—just as it had been designed nearly one hundred years ago. Weathered, barren land—beaten down by the wind and waves—lay on either side of the structure before being met by the strong and ferocious ocean.

Their friend Austin had been hired to fix it up, and Cassidy and Ty had been here more than once and for more than one reason. When the place was restored, it would no doubt become an island hot spot.

Cassidy and Ty remained in the truck with the windows down, not bothering to get out. The scent of the salty sea drifted in, and even though they were a good five hundred feet away from the ocean, its mighty waves still could be heard pounding the shore.

Ty opened the door and let Kujo jump out. The faithful dog bounded on the nearby sand, chasing birds and hunting down sand crabs.

"What's going on?" Ty turned toward her, his full attention on the conversation.

Cassidy filled him in, sharing what Ryan had told her, classified or not. She trusted Ty with her life, and Ty already knew most of it . . . except maybe about Samuel's possible involvement.

"He thinks you need to leave?" Ty repeated.

"Ryan thinks if he found me, anyone can." Cassidy's words sounded dull and lifeless, even to her own ears.

"He could be right." Ty's voice cracked.

Cassidy scooted closer. "I don't want to leave."

"We've both known the day could come when you might have to."

The pressure on her shoulders bent her forward, felt like too much to hold up on her own. "I don't know what to do."

"Come here." Ty pulled her into his arms and tucked Cassidy's head beneath his chin. "We'll figure it out."

We'll. She loved how Ty was in this with her. How she was his priority.

How could she leave that behind?

Maybe she didn't have to.

She pulled back and locked gazes with him. "Maybe we could all go. You, me, and Kujo."

"And do what?"

She shrugged and shook her head, desperate to find the right answer. "Stay in hiding until the trial."

"What if it's postponed?"

"Then we keep hiding."

Ty didn't say anything for a minute. But when he turned back toward her, his eyes were full of emotion. "Is that what you really want to do?"

Was it? Was running the wise thing?

Cassidy rubbed her temples. "I . . . I don't know. I wish I did."

Ty caressed her hair away from her face. "Then let's not do anything rash. Let's think this through."

Did she even have time to think things through? The

pressure of the situation built in her until she felt ready to explode. "They got to Samuel, Ty. They got to *Samuel*. He was the inside man. I don't know how they persuaded him or what his motive might have been, but Ryan thinks he was working for DH-7."

"That's a lot to comprehend."

"How could I not have seen it?"

"I'm sorry, Cassidy."

Cassidy closed her eyes and leaned into Ty again, trying to process everything that had happened. Maybe she was thinking too hard, and that was her problem. Maybe she just needed to take a step back and clear her head.

She popped her eyes open and turned toward him, remembering there were other things going on here besides her problems—other important things. "How's your mom, Ty?"

His face went from tense to ashen. "She's . . . she's okay. The surgery went well. They'll do another round of chemo and see if they can get the rest of the cancer."

"But how is she otherwise? Mentally? Emotionally?" Cassidy knew there was so much more to the disease than its physical effects.

"My mom's a strong woman. She's staying positive. And she knows if it's the good Lord's time to take her, she's ready to go. The problem is that the rest of us aren't ready."

Cassidy squeezed his hand, wishing she could do something to help. Wishing life had a button one could push that would make everything better. That was just frivolous, wishful thinking. "I know you're not. I'm so sorry. But I'm glad you were able to be there for her."

"Me too. She sends her love." He reached into his pocket. "And this."

Cassidy stared at the object in his hands, squinting as the sun glinted off the clear gemstone. "A ring?"

Ty studied it also, his eyes warming. "It was my grandmother's."

She stared at the gold band embellished with three diamonds and a smattering of stardust around it. "It's beautiful."

He turned toward her, the warmth in his eyes saturated with love and concern. "I want it to be yours."

Cassidy could hardly breathe. Had she heard correctly? "What?"

"I know this is horrible timing. But there just never seems to be a good time, and I don't want to waste any opportunities. Cassidy, you know I want to marry you. I want to make it official." He held out the ring, offering it to her as a promise of his forever intentions.

Moisture filled her eyes as his words washed over her.

Be with Ty.

Forever.

Nothing sounded better.

"You already know my answer," she said, her voice a wisp of what it usually was.

Emotions pummeled her. Elated joy mixed with agonizing anxiety. Joy because Ty was whom she'd always wanted. Anxiety because her life didn't lend itself to a happily ever after right now, and she wasn't sure when that would change.

Or if it ever would.

Ty slipped the ring on her finger. It fit perfectly, almost as if it was made for her.

Cassidy stared at the jewelry for a moment. It was the most beautiful thing she'd ever seen.

She leaned forward and kissed Ty. Really kissed him. Kissed him in a way that made her forget about all of her problems—for a few minutes, at least. She'd take whatever she could get—whatever sliver of happiness was offered.

When they pulled apart, Cassidy rested her head on Ty's shoulder, realizing more than ever just how much was at stake here.

"Maybe we *should* run," Ty said softly.

Running was so tempting.

But it was never quite that easy, was it? Because your past always caught up. Her life right now was a case in point.

"I don't want to run forever," she said.

"So what do you want to do?"

That was a good question. When Cassidy pushed everything else aside, what was that answer? What would her life look like? She stared out the window a moment, stared at the white-capped waves in the distance as she contemplated her answer.

"I want to stand my ground," she muttered. "Am I crazy?"

"Never."

"I don't want to get anyone else hurt." So many people Cassidy cared about had their lives turned upside down for her. No more. Enough was enough.

"I'm a big boy. Don't worry about me."

"You've already put so much into Hope House." Ty was converting his cottage into a veteran's retreat center. However, someone had set the place on fire a week ago and stalled progress. Now that Ty was back, he would no doubt begin working on it again . . . except Cassidy was curtailing his plans . . . again. "You've worked so hard to get this far on it."

"Hope House is in God's hands," Ty said. "When it's supposed to happen—where it's supposed to happen—it will. He opens and shuts the doors as He needs to."

Before they could talk anymore, Cassidy's phone rang. It was Ryan.

"I took a power nap, and I'm feeling more rested," he started.

"Good to know."

"Listen, I know I said I would give you time, but could we eat an early dinner together? I feel like we still have a lot to talk about."

Cassidy glanced at Ty, hoping he would understand. "We can have dinner, but only if Ty is there."

"I expected as much." The dull tone of Ryan's voice indicated he wasn't entirely happy with the clause.

"How about if you come to my house? I can pick up some food." Cassidy glanced at her watch and saw it was already two o'clock. The past few hours had passed quickly—too quickly.

"Okay, I'll be there." Ryan paused. "And I really need you to think about what I said earlier. Leaving this place is your best choice, whether you want to admit it or not."

CHAPTER
FOUR

TY AND CASSIDY stopped at the Crazy Chefette, a restaurant owned by their friend Lisa Garth. She was known for her weird food combinations, and the scent of Old Bay and cinnamon mingling in the air only reminded Ty of all the crazy recipes Lisa developed.

He paused at the door, and his heart twisted with grief for a moment.

This place seemed like such a part of his life here with Cassidy.

Could that all really be on the line?

This place—Lantern Beach—just wouldn't be the same without Cassidy. If she left . . . everywhere he went would be a reminder of what they'd had together. What they should have together. Here on this island they both loved.

The thought of her leaving left him with the intense reminder that life wasn't fair.

His thoughts clashed together inside him until a dull headache developed.

Ty nodded across the room at his friend Jimmy James, who was eating a Heart Attack Burger—one with three hamburger patties, bacon, cheese, a fried egg, and a split hotdog. The man wiped a glob of mayonnaise from his chin and waved back.

Ty and Cassidy met Lisa at the counter. Lisa finished instructing the cashier on something before turning to them with a bright smile. "Hey, you two! What brings you by?"

"We need to pick up some food to go." Cassidy's voice cracked, belying the tension she was desperately trying to hide.

"You're not going to stay and eat with us?" Lisa absently straightened some menus as they talked.

"I wish we could," Cassidy said. "But we need to take it back to my place. I have . . . company."

Lisa's eyebrows shot up before wiggling with curiosity. "Company? Sounds intriguing."

"It's not," Cassidy said, her lips pulling down at the corners. "Not really."

A surge of irritation rushed through Ty's blood, and he fisted his hands. Every time he pictured Ryan's smug little face, he wanted to punch someone. Punching someone wasn't a reaction he wanted. No, self-control was important to him.

But the man was a living, breathing jerk. Maybe he'd come here with good intentions—intentions of helping Cassidy. That still didn't mean Ty liked him, though.

"Hey, you guys!" Skye joined them at the counter, her bangle bracelets clanging together like windchimes on her wrists. "What's going on? You selling ice cream down at the fishing tournament today, Cassidy?"

"Not today," Cassidy said. "I thought about it, but something popped up."

This conversation seemed so normal in comparison to everything that was happening. Ty's heart thudded at the thought. It sounded like nothing had changed, when in reality everything could change.

He could hardly stomach the thought.

"Well, both of you look like you've just seen a ghost," Skye said. The woman was a little too insightful for her own good sometimes.

"Just having one of those days," Cassidy said.

Lisa's gaze focused on Cassidy's hand, and she let out a squeal. "Oh my goodness! Is that what I think it is?"

Cassidy glanced down and smiled. "It is. Ty and I are . . ."

"Getting married," Ty finished.

Lisa and Skye both squealed this time, and a round of hugs went around.

"I'm so happy for you two." Skye smiled, but there was a certain sadness in her gaze—a sadness she never wanted to talk about.

"I can't wait to plan the menu!" Lisa said before her smile slipped. "Provided you want me to, of course."

"We'd love for you to help," Cassidy said.

"And we should have a little party to celebrate," Lisa continued. "How about tonight?"

Cassidy and Ty exchanged a glance.

"Not tonight," Ty said. "But sometime soon."

"It's a deal," Lisa said. She leaned with her elbows against the counter, almost like she had all the time in the world. "Did I mention how excited I am?"

Ty smiled. This was what he loved about being part of a strong community—sharing your successes and joys with other people.

"Guess what?" Lisa continued. "Not to change the subject, but . . . Ernestine came in here yesterday. Can you believe it?"

Ernestine was the local newspaper editor, and she was also agoraphobic. Seeing her overcome her fears was pretty amazing. She'd made some impressive strides lately.

"That's great," Ty said.

He glanced at Cassidy and noted how pale she looked. He squeezed her hand, and she sent him a small, almost apologetic smile.

Ty knew Cassidy wanted to be open with her friends about this hidden part of her life. But it wouldn't be wise. Only he and Mac knew her secret, and it needed to stay that way.

"So, what do you have for us?" Ty asked. "Anything family style?"

"I just made some Kool-Aid pickles." Lisa reached

below the counter and held up a jar of red pickle spears. "They're really tasty."

Cassidy's nose scrunched. "Maybe something a little more substantial?"

"A bologna cake?"

Ty's stomach churned at the sound of it. "What is that?"

"It's delicious. You can cut slices—just like cake—and dip crackers into it as a spread. I pipe cheese all over it, which makes it look like a cake. Isn't that cool?"

Cassidy didn't say anything for a moment until, "Anything else?"

"Seafood lasagna soup and Old Bay bread?"

"We'll take that," Cassidy said.

"And I made some fried milk for dessert. Have you ever tried it? It's delicious." Lisa ran her tongue along her lips, like a kid getting ice cream.

"I've never had it, but I'll take your word for it," Cassidy said. "Add some of that too."

"Perfect!" Lisa smiled enthusiastically. "I'll go pack it up for you. It's going to be a winner. I promise."

Ty ran his hand along Cassidy's back before pulling her closer.

He didn't like where this situation was going.

And he felt powerless to do anything about it.

At her house, Cassidy wasted no time getting things cleaned up—and it felt good to stay busy. She opened the windows to continue airing the place out since the faint smell of smoke still lingered in the air. She also pulled out another place setting for Ryan.

While she did that, Ty called Mac and asked him to check the security footage from the station. Cassidy wanted a visual on who had come in. With every second that ticked by, the situation felt more and more burdensome.

"You look nervous." Ty hung up and began scraping the burnt quiche into the trashcan while Cassidy pulled out the fruit salad and muffins from breakfast.

"I am. I'm sorry. It's just that—"

"You were engaged to Ryan."

She paused and nodded. "But you're the one I'm in love with. Always. I just dread the awkwardness."

Ty turned toward the sink and began washing the quiche plate for her. "You never really talked about what happened between the two of you. Is there anything I should know?"

How much should she say? Cassidy didn't make it a habit of talking about her past relationships with her current relationship. But her life felt exceedingly complicated right now with so many threads going in so many different directions, almost like being emotionally drawn and quartered.

"We met when he worked for the prosecuting attorney, and I was a detective." Cassidy pulled some ice trays from the freezer, needing to do something with her hands as she talked. "We started dating only a couple of months prior to me going undercover. Before I took the assignment with DH-7, he proposed."

Should she mention that their relationship had been kept a secret? No, she decided. She didn't bring up that detail.

In retrospect, it should have been the writing on the wall. But sometimes love—or what a person thought was love—made them blind to the truth.

"He proposed, and you said yes." Ty didn't glance at her; he just continued doing the dishes.

It didn't surprise her. Did any guy really want to know the details of their fiancée's past love life? Yet parts of it were important to share simply for perspective.

Cassidy drew in a heavy breath. "I did say yes. Looking back, it was mostly because we made sense. Ryan was so much like my father—someone who was driven completely by his job. I was so goal-oriented that I thought the match would be perfect."

Sometimes people gravitated toward what they knew—even if what they knew wasn't desirable. Cassidy wasn't an expert, but she'd observed that in her own life and in the lives of others.

"So what happened?"

She finished filling the glasses with ice, crossed her arms, and leaned against the kitchen counter. "A couple things. First, I realized that he didn't miss me. I realized while I was undercover how many changes I needed to make in my life. I didn't want to end up like my dad. I want my life to revolve around the people I love, not money and career."

"I see." Ty finished washing the pie plate and moved on to a mixing bowl.

"We made sense on paper. But I just wanted more in my life. I want someone I can't live without, not someone I think I can make it work with."

"Sounds wise." He put the bowl into the rack by the sink and dried his hands with a dish towel.

Cassidy's heart filled with love when she looked at him. He was strong but humble. Protective but respectful. Confident but kind.

And he did dishes.

What more could she want?

"And I met you, and I realized what I'd been missing," she said quietly.

"I definitely like the sound of that." A smile played across Ty's lips as he stepped closer. His hands slipped around her waist, and he tugged her closer. "Let's get married sooner rather than later."

His words washed over her. Had she heard correctly? "How soon are you thinking?"

"As soon as this situation is resolved. When Ryan's gone. When you're safe. Why waste any time? I'm not going to change my mind."

She loved the sound of that. If only these things were that simple. "We've talked about the legalities and challenges of getting married right now—especially since I'm using an alias."

"We can figure out something."

Cassidy smiled, warmth spreading through her when she heard the sincerity and dedication in Ty's voice. "I do love that confidence."

Ty's lips quickly brushed hers, but when he pulled back, the inquiry was still in his gaze. "So?"

She let out a laugh, the ring on her finger bringing a dash of delight to this otherwise trying situation. "So, as soon as this mess is over, let's do it. Let's find a way to make it happen. Because I'm not changing my mind either."

A grin spread across his face. "It's a deal."

Before they could talk anymore, someone knocked at the door.

Ryan had arrived.

***

"You look refreshed," Cassidy told Ryan as he stepped inside. He'd changed into a clean outfit, one nearly identical to his earlier one. His thick hair was still in place. And based on his scent, he'd shaved.

Cassidy could smell his aftershave as soon as he walked into a room.

"I do feel better." Ryan's gaze went across the room, and he nodded curtly at Ty, who mirrored the action.

Meanwhile, Kujo sat beside Cassidy, just daring Ryan to make a wrong move.

This was going to be fun. But having Ty with her was the only solution Cassidy felt comfortable with—and comfort was really a relative term at this point.

"Why don't we all sit down? The food is nothing fancy, but it's ready," Cassidy said, instantly slipping back into her role as a hostess. All of her etiquette training seemed to be coming back, and the laid-back beach girl seemed to slip further away.

She didn't want to waste time with formalities. There was too much at stake. Too much to talk about.

How much about her theories could she tell Ryan? Could she trust him with everything she'd learned?

Probably. Apparently, Samuel was the one Cassidy shouldn't have been trusting this whole time. The real-ization still caused her heart to lurch.

They sat at the table—awkwardly, of course—and passed the food around. Ryan made small talk, chatting about the inn where he was staying and mentioning how beautiful the island was. The scent of the seafood lasagna soup drifted up around them, as did the coffee that Cassidy had started earlier. She'd even dug into the secret stash she'd ordered from Seattle.

Ryan's eyes latched onto her hand. "You're . . . engaged."

Cassidy glanced at the ring on her finger. "I am."

"I guess I should say congratulations." His voice sounded anything but congratulatory, though.

Her throat was tight as she muttered, "Thank you."

Ryan hadn't given her a ring when they were engaged. No, he'd said he would do that later, once they were free to speak about their relationship. In other words, after he was elected.

She took a sip of her soup, unusually nervous about

this conversation but ready to change the subject from her engagement. "So, everything is lined up for the trial?"

"We just need you there." Ryan took a drink of his water. "Did you hear we were able to move up the date?"

"Samuel mentioned that last time we talked."

"We've done great work, Cad—" He paused and shook his head, letting out a chuckle that seemed too uptight to be sincere. "Cassidy. I don't know how I'll get used to saying that. You'll always be Cady to me."

At the intimate tone of his voice, Cassidy knew she had to change the subject. She squared her shoulders and lowered her spoon. "You said all of Samuel's evidence disappeared with him?"

Ryan nodded. "That's right. It appears he's been planning this for a long time."

"But why? Why would he do this? Was he the puppet master the whole time?" That was what Cassidy didn't understand. What could Samuel's motive possibly be?

"The puppet master?"

She cleared her throat, realizing she needed to clarify her statement. "That's what I call the man in charge. I realized a few weeks ago that there had to be someone above Raul. Someone who put this bounty on my head."

"Why would you think that?"

"Orion was obviously answering to a higher authority. I just didn't realize it was Samuel."

Ryan nodded slowly and wiped his mouth. "You're right. We have suspected that, and we were trying to nail down who this person was. After your first safe house was attacked, we knew there had to be a leak. We've been investigating since then."

"But you never suspected it was Samuel?"

"Not until he came into the office last week acting strangely. I think he was getting spooked, that he was afraid you were getting too close to the truth."

"But if he wasn't discovered, why blow his cover?" Cassidy asked. "You said he disappeared, right?"

"That's correct."

"And you assumed it was because he was involved with DH-7."

"I began digging, and, yes, that's how it appears."

"Why? Why would he get involved?"

Ryan shrugged. "I don't know the answers, Cassidy."

"And why would he get himself involved with a group like DH-7? He had a good career, a good life, a good family."

"Money, power, greed—once you have some, you only want more. It can infect the unlikeliest of people."

"I agree—the lure of those things is strong. I just never saw that as important to Samuel."

"I'm sorry, Cassidy." Ryan started to reach for her hand but stopped himself. "I know this has to be hard on you."

Her stomach clenched at the compassion in his voice. She didn't want Ryan's compassion. She wanted answers. She wanted understanding. She didn't want sympathy.

Just then, her phone buzzed. She glanced at her screen and saw that it was a text from Mac.

"Excuse me a minute," Cassidy muttered before clicking on the message.

Mac had taken a screenshot of the security footage showing the man who'd come in earlier today. Cassidy studied the image. The man was just as Quinton had described him. Medium height. Light brown hair.

It definitely wasn't Samuel or Ricky. The man looked vaguely familiar, but she couldn't place him.

After a second of hesitation, she showed the picture to Ryan. "Do you recognize this man?"

Recognition spread across his features. "As a matter of fact, I do. That's Greg Marks. He and Samuel worked together."

CHAPTER
FIVE

AFTER THEY ATE, everyone stood. Ty had been quiet—he'd been mostly listening. Every so often, Cassidy had noticed him scanning the windows, looking for any sign of trouble.

Ryan paused by the door before leaving, something obviously on his mind. "It's more urgent than ever that you make a choice. Especially if Greg is on the island. That means that Samuel could be here also. Until we know if he's been captured, you're not safe."

Ty stepped closer. "I'll keep an eye on her."

Ryan's gaze flickered with annoyance, as if he didn't appreciate Ty's intrusion. "You're not supposed to know any of this. And I don't know what Cassidy told you, but I'm not sure you really realize how ruthless these men are."

"I've faced terrorists." Ty said the words casually, like there was nothing unusual about what he'd done in his past. In truth, he was a hero, and he'd risked his life to preserve the freedoms of strangers and for his country.

Ryan said nothing, but the agitation in his eyes grew. His gaze flickered back to Cassidy, dismissing Ty's statement with the one action. "Tomorrow morning?"

Cassidy nodded, still feeling dazed and a little irritated. "I'll let you know then."

But she already knew what her choice was. She was staying on Lantern Beach with Ty and Kujo.

Before Ryan stepped out the door, she had another question for him. "Ryan, does the expression Tango Mango mean anything to you?"

He narrowed his eyes. "Is that military jargon or something?"

She didn't want him to know that Samuel had sent her information—top secret documents—that included memos between the leaders of DH-7. The gang had operated as more of a business than she'd ever guessed.

One of the code names they'd used for a scientist they'd hired was Tango Mango.

"I thought I heard Raul use that phrase once," she finally said, leaving out part of the details.

"You never mentioned that when you were debriefed." Ryan studied her expression, almost like he wanted to jump into trial mode and put her on the witness stand under oath. "I've reread those interviews with you many times."

"Maybe I blocked it out. I'm not sure. It just came back to me, though."

His shoulders softened, and he rolled his neck—all in a few seconds—and then he snapped back to professional mode. "If I come across anything about it, I can let you know. But I don't understand why you'd want to know that information or what you think this has to do with this case."

The response was on the tip of Cassidy's tongue. But she didn't speak it out loud. Not to Ryan. Not until she knew if she was crazy or not.

"It's just been bugging me," she finally said. "That's all."

Ryan's gaze lingered on her another moment until he finally nodded. "I wish you'd leave. Now. You're no good to us dead."

This wasn't really about Cassidy. No, it was about what she could do for the prosecution. It had become clear to her that she was just a pawn in this whole investigation. Then again, Cassidy had felt like a pawn for most of her life, a figurehead for her parents and family.

Being in Lantern Beach was the first time she'd felt like a person. Like a friend. A girlfriend.

"Bye, Ryan," she muttered.

He gave her a nod and then stepped out.

As soon as the door closed and Ryan's steps descended the stairs, Ty turned toward Cassidy. His expression looked hard. "I don't like him."

Cassidy hadn't expected them to be best friends, so his words were no surprise. "Is it because I used to be engaged to him?"

His jaw flexed, and he drew in a deep breath. "Because he seems like the type who likes trophies."

Cassidy couldn't argue, but it brought her a strange comfort to know that Ty had seen that in Ryan. If only Cassidy had seen it earlier. "Ryan is out of my life. Mostly. After the trial he will be."

"You didn't tell him your theory." Ty paused. "About Tango Mango. Do you think he's involved?"

"Sometimes I think it's just better to keep information close until I'm sure it's the right time to expose it," Cassidy said. "I'm not sure today is that day."

"If your theory is true, then this is even bigger than you anticipated."

Cassidy crossed her arms, wishing they could talk about something else. But there wasn't time to spare. And Ty's words were true. With every new detail she uncovered, she realized just how huge this whole web of crime was.

"I know. The truth is, I think Lucy's dad was involved in DH-7, and that involvement somehow got my friend killed." She paused. "I don't think it was a coincidence I was chosen for this undercover assignment, either. I think someone was pulling the strings from the start."

"Why do you think that?"

There was only one theory that stood out in her mind. "Maybe because my father is one of the richest men in the United States."

"Could be true. The lengths people will go to for money are mind blowing."

Cassidy's phone buzzed again, and again it was Mac.

Can you meet me out on the boardwalk? I can't leave, but we need to talk. Face to face.

She glanced up at Ty. "What do you think? Is it safe?"

"I don't think anywhere is safe. But I've got your back."

Cassidy and Ty easily found Mac on the boardwalk. He stood near the railing separating the sidewalk from the sand, staring at the beach, and eating . . . popcorn.

Cassidy smiled. She loved the man's gumption. On some people, his attitude might be irritating. But his humor fit Mac, making him charming and entertaining.

As they approached, she noted how nice it was to see him in his police uniform—where he belonged. He lived for stuff like this and would be excellent as a permanent police chief, even though he didn't want the job. He claimed that, at sixty, he was too old.

In the background, near the shore, a row of fishermen cast their lines into the water, hoping for a prize for the best fish. The surf was rough today, and forecasters had promised a storm later tonight. Rip current advisories had already been posted up and down the shore.

It was busier on the boardwalk than Cassidy would have guessed, but she supposed the fishermen had brought their families. Some carried cotton candy, others carried cups of peel-and-eat shrimp or paper boats of boardwalk fries. It seemed like the quintessential beach day.

Mac glanced over, saw them approaching, and tossed the rest of his popcorn in a nearby garbage bin. "Already broke up three fights, and lifeguards have rescued four people from this surf. I'd say it doesn't get much more exciting around here."

Cassidy frowned. "Those things might not be your biggest problems of the day, unfortunately."

His smile dipped, and his joking disappeared. "Who's that man on the video?"

Ty squeezed in closer to her, and Cassidy knew he was watching everything around them. It was good to have another set of eyes on the situation—and on her.

Cassidy explained today's events, and, as she did, Mac's expression grew darker and darker.

"Something doesn't sound right," he said.

"I'm torn between staying and leaving," Cassidy admitted. "I want to stay, but I don't want to be stupid."

"At least here the environment is controlled—for the most part. We know this island and can keep an eye on who comes and goes. If you leave and trouble follows you . . ."

"I'll be on my own." As the words hit her ears, Cassidy cringed. She hated the sound of that.

"Exactly." Mac glanced around. "I'll keep my eyes open for the man from the video. At least Quinton didn't show that he had no common sense when the man asked about you. Sometimes, I think that was Bozoman's prerequisite for hiring anyone. Are you competent? What's that mean? Perfect—you're hired!"

Cassidy smiled. Bozoman—better known as Alan Bozeman—had been the police chief, but he'd stepped down to deal with some family issues. It was probably better that way since the man had not only been inexperienced, but also clueless.

"But I don't like the idea that this man is in town," Mac continued.

"Believe me—I don't either. It's like the trouble doesn't stop coming."

In a split second, the air changed around them. Cassidy felt it, felt the goosebumps pop up on her skin and her hairs rise.

"Cassidy, get down!" Ty shouted.

Before Cassidy could react, Ty threw himself over her.

A gunshot filled the air, followed by screams from the people around her.

CHAPTER
SIX

STILL USING his own body to shield Cassidy, Ty glanced back up to the rooftop where he'd spotted the shooter. He'd seen the glint of the gun's scope—just a split second before the man had fired.

But now the shooter was gone.

That didn't mean he was going to get away. Not if Ty had anything to do with it.

First, he looked down at Cassidy beneath him. She'd hit the boardwalk—but at least she hadn't taken a bullet. "Are you okay?"

She pushed herself up on her elbows, looking slightly dazed. "Yeah, I'm fine."

"Stay here," Ty said. "Mac, can you stay with her?"

"For a few minutes while I call in backup." Mac knelt beside her, ready to help her to her feet.

Ty took off toward the yellow building housing a candy shop on the first floor. The second floor was probably an apartment, if he had to guess, and the whole thing had a flat roof—perfect for a wannabe sniper.

He needed to cut the shooter off before he got away.

He dodged tourists and fishermen and a young couple from church who were strolling and eating ice cream. Some people stopped to stare. Some had run for cover. Some simply thought the noise signaled the start of a new round in the fishing tournament—based on a conversation Ty overheard.

He had to catch this guy. If he did, Cassidy would be one step closer to freedom. Not to mention that he and Cassidy would be one step closer to being able to get married.

Vendors made the area even tighter—people selling homemade soap and spice rubs and other things Ty didn't have time to look at. They lined the edges of the quaint walkway.

As he rounded the edge of a line of shops, he spotted someone jumping from a ladder on the side of the building. That had to be the shooter.

The man wore a baseball cap pulled down low, so Ty couldn't see his face. He just knew he was a white man of average height and weight. He could be the man from the police station—Greg, Ryan had told them.

The crowds still scattered all around him, obstacles in his way of catching the man. He skirted around people as fast as he could, trying to reach the shooter.

His legs burned as he chased after the man. The shooter had too much of a head start.

That meant Ty needed to push himself harder.

The man glanced back—a potentially fatal mistake because he lost time.

Ty watched as he turned into an alley. If the man was hoping to cut through to the beach, he was sadly mistaken. This alley ended at a fence.

And it was Ty's chance to catch him and find out what was going on here.

Ty turned the corner. Just as he did, something hard smashed into his head.

Cassidy stood and rubbed her elbow. She was going to have a bruise there—maybe even a small scrape. But those were the least of her concerns right now.

She swung her head around, searching for any destruction the bullet had caused. Anyone hurt. Anything destroyed.

She spotted a bullet hole in the wooden railing within arm's distance of her. This situation could have turned out so much differently. Someone could have been killed or seriously injured.

Thank goodness the man had missed.

But her heart pounded so hard she could hear it, half expected even to see it pulsing at her chest cavity just like in those old cartoons.

Mac still had one hand on her arm, but the other hand gripped his phone. He hung up and slid the device back into his pocket. "Backup is on the way—if you consider Quinton and Wheezer backup. Are you okay?"

"I'm fine. Really. Go. Go help Ty. You can't stay here and babysit me."

"But—"

"I have my gun." She sounded more breathless than she'd like. "I'll be okay."

Mac hesitated one more moment before taking off. They needed to catch whoever had done this.

Cassidy didn't plan on sitting back while everyone else did the dangerous work either.

After catching her breath, she rushed toward the scene, desperate to see something. To help. To find Ty.

As she sprinted, she scanned everything around her. People ran for cover or huddled together. A sense of panic fell around her.

"Someone is shooting!" a woman yelled.

More chaos broke out. People ran. Hid. Looked for loved ones.

Cassidy didn't know where the man had gone or what he even looked like. But she felt certain she'd know who he was when she saw him. That she'd sense the adrenaline that must be coming off him like heat waves off asphalt after pulling that trigger.

She reached the end of the block but saw no one.

Stopping, Cassidy let out a sigh.

Where had the man gone? Where was Ty? Had he caught the shooter?

She looped back around, trying to catch up with Mac and Ty before they got worried. As she reached the other end of the row of shops, Ty appeared from around the corner. He rubbed his head, his eyes narrowed and maybe even disoriented.

Cassidy rushed toward him, a surge of worry rising in her. "Are you okay? What happened?"

"I thought I had him." He glanced around like he might find the man. "But when I rounded the corner, he slammed a broken four-by-four into my head."

"Oh, Ty." She studied his face. A small bump had already formed near his temple, and a red mark blotched his skin.

He dropped his hand, and his gaze came back into focus. "I'm fine. Just my pride is injured."

"I guess he got away?" Cassidy had allowed hope to momentarily enter her thoughts—hope that they'd catch this guy and put all of this behind them. The thought had been foolish.

Ty frowned and looked off in the distance, as if remembering the moment. "That's right. Unfortunately."

"Did you get a glimpse of him?"

"Nothing definite. He wore a hat. But it could have been Greg."

"Maybe we should have you checked out." Worst-case scenarios rushed through her mind. Head injuries were nothing to play with.

"I'm really fine." Ty squeezed Cassidy's arm now, his gaze firm and leaving no room for questions.

Cassidy stared beyond Ty a moment, her thoughts

racing to review what had happened. "Why would someone open fire in public?"

It was such a risky move. Bystanders could have been injured or killed.

"Someone wanted to send a message," Ty said.

"You're right. Maybe someone saw something. Mac's out there now investigating. The good news is that no one was hurt."

"Maybe we should get you home." Ty put his arm around her.

"That's a good idea." Cassidy took the keys from his hands. "But I'm driving."

CHAPTER
SEVEN

BACK AT CASSIDY'S HOUSE, Kujo greeted them as soon as they opened the door. Cassidy patted his head but didn't step inside.

She had to be overly careful here and to live like her life was on the line.

Because it was.

As if Ty could read her thoughts, he strode down the hallway, beating her to the task of checking the space for intruders.

"It's clear," he announced, joining her again at the entryway.

"Thank goodness." Cassidy studied the knot on his forehead, worry twisting inside her. "Are you sure you're okay?"

"I promise. I'm fine. If I'm not, I'll go to the clinic. I'm just glad *you're* okay."

That was Ty for you. Always thinking of her.

Cassidy knew he wouldn't change his mind about

going to be checked out, so she moved on. She'd call him out on it later if the injury still seemed to be bothering him.

"I studied the area on the boardwalk where the bullet hit," Cassidy said, grabbing bottles of water for both of them. "It was only a foot away from where I was standing. If I was the target, either the guy has bad aim, or he missed on purpose."

"Maybe he was trying to scare you."

She sat down on the couch, pulling Ty beside her. What a day. Her head was already pounding, and to say she was on edge would be an understatement. Every time she turned around, she expected to see someone there, an unknown face full of vengeance, ready to kill her.

"I tried to do some research on Greg Marks earlier," Cassidy started. "But there's nothing on him. In fact, that's probably not his real name. Ryan claims he works with law enforcement in some capacity, but without calling my contacts, I can't confirm that."

"Should we ask Mac to report him?"

Cassidy shook her head. "I thought about that. But it will send the feds here. It will only bring more attention to Lantern Beach and . . ."

"To you," Ty finished.

"That's right. I feel like my hands are tied."

"We'll think of something."

Cassidy reached for Lucy's calendar, which was always a source of comfort. It sat on the end table beside her couch. But Cassidy froze when she looked down at it.

"What is it?" Ty asked.

She stared at the magazines on her end table. They were mostly tourist booklets that the cottage owner had left, each filled with coupons and advertisements cleverly disguised as articles.

"The stack seems different," she said. "It's . . . straight."

"Aren't they always straight?"

Cassidy didn't quite know how to word it. "Well, yes. But not this straight. I know that sounds weird. Maybe it's just the stress of the day getting to me."

"If someone broke in just to straighten up your magazines, then they've got an interesting hobby going on."

Cassidy stood, her instincts blazing. "I just want to look around one more time."

Ty followed her lead. "I'll go with you."

She pulled out her gun, just in case. And then Cassidy wandered through her house again. Had someone been in here? Or was she just paranoid? It was hard to tell, and her emotions didn't make it any easier.

She checked each of the rooms before ending in the kitchen. She checked the cabinets and the silverware drawer. Nothing. Finally she opened the drawer below the phone—where she kept her stash of guns in a false bottom.

The papers inside—a phone book, some menus from

local restaurants, a notebook containing a list of groceries she needed to buy—were all straightened and looked immaculately organized. But her guns were still there.

Had Cassidy done this? Had she gone looking for something and absent-mindedly straightened the contents of the drawer?

It was the only thing that made sense.

Yet it didn't.

"Well?" Ty stopped behind her.

"Maybe everything is getting to me." She pressed her hands against the counter. She wanted to believe her words were true. She really did.

"Maybe. But you have good instincts. One thing I learned in the battlefield was to never ignore those reflexes."

She nibbled on her lip a moment, needing to think this through a little more. "Why would someone come in to my house and straighten papers?"

"Maybe they were looking for something and tried to tidy up so you couldn't tell."

Her blood felt even colder. Ty could be right.

Cassidy's phone rang and snapped her from her thoughts. And that ring indicated it wasn't her regular phone. No, it was her secret phone. The one that usually only Samuel called on.

She fished it from her purse and sucked in a deep breath.

Was she reading the number correctly?

"Who is it?" Ty asked.

Cassidy glanced up and met his gaze, her heart thumping into her rib cage. "It's Lucy's mom."

Cassidy hadn't expected this. Hadn't expected that a plan she'd set in motion three days ago might actually work.

What she'd done had been risky—maybe too risky.

But the payoff had seemed worth it, and she'd been desperate. Maybe even foolish.

Cassidy put the phone to her ear.

"Hello?" Cassidy's voice trembled with anticipation.

"Cady?" Mae's voice stretched across the line, tinged with confusion and curiosity.

Hearing Mae say her real name sucked her back in time to her old life. "It's me."

"You're . . . okay."

"Yes, I am. For now. You can't tell anyone about this call."

"That works . . . because you can't tell anyone about what I have to tell you, either."

Cassidy's pulse spiked. Was this the conversation that she'd been wanting to have for months now? "I can do that."

Mae let out a soft sigh, like she struggled with the ramifications of this phone call. "I . . . I know I shouldn't be talking to you. But I have to. I have things to tell you."

Cassidy clutched the phone tighter and paced toward the window. "What is it, Mae?"

"It's about that night you asked me about before I hung up on you." Her voice cracked.

"The one in February? The year Lucy died?" There'd been a page missing from Lucy's calendar, only Cassidy hadn't realized it until she'd ordered a replica. She was just following a hunch here—but sometimes hunches could lead to answers.

"That's right." Mae let out another sigh. "It was a bad night, Cady. I don't have much time before Hiroto returns, so I'm going to have to be quick. There was a big fight that evening."

"Involving Lucy?"

"No, between my husband and me. I was afraid he'd become involved in something less than honorable. He'd been acting strangely, and I demanded answers. I was tired of it—tired of the secrets. He told me to be quiet and just comply, for the sake of everyone involved."

Lucy had mentioned there were some problems at home. Maybe she hadn't delved into the full extent of just how bad things were. "I can understand how that may have been difficult, but why would Lucy rip that day out?"

"She was upset, but we begged her not to mention it to anyone. Even to you. I later went into her room and found that page crumbled on the floor. I think she had a harder time that night than she wanted to let on. She feared her father and I would get divorced. She told me she'd never seen her dad so upset. Neither had I, to be honest." Mae's voice trailed off with unspoken emotion.

"Do you know what was wrong?" Cassidy turned away, needing for a moment to block out Ty so she could focus on this conversation. Still, Cassidy could sense him close behind her and at the ready if she needed him.

"I think someone was threatening him. Of course, you know what happened three days later." Mae's voice cracked. "Lucy died. She was in my room that night. She'd had a nightmare. After she fell back to sleep, I went into the study. I hardly ever did that, but I just needed to clear my head. I fell asleep in a chair there."

"I see." Cassidy remembered those details but didn't rush Mae.

"It was supposed to be me, Cody." A sob escaped, a sob that turned into a wreck of emotions and tears and wailing. "I was supposed to die that night, not Lucy."

Cassidy waited a few minutes, trying to murmur words of comfort. But were there any in a situation like this?

When Mae's cries calmed, Cassidy asked, "Are you sure it was supposed to be you?"

"Nearly certain."

Cassidy squeezed the phone harder. All she could hear was her heart thump, thump, thumping in her chest. "Did you tell the police that?"

"No. I knew how it would look. I mean, I told them how I got up from bed, but not about the fight within the family. I didn't want to believe that my husband might have had anything to do with our daughter's death."

"But now you do? What changed your mind?"

Silence stretched, and Cassidy feared Mae might hang up. She stared out the window, waiting and praying this wasn't the end of the conversation. She still needed more information.

"He has secret meetings. Men stop by the house when Hiroto thinks I'm sleeping, but my husband refuses to talk about it. He just says he's doing what he has to do, and unless I want to cause more trouble, I should mind my own business."

That didn't sound good—at all. Cassidy remembered Hiroto as being such a gentle, quiet man. "What do you think is going on? Certainly you have a theory."

All these years should have given Mae plenty of time to think about it.

"I think someone is holding a gun to him, making him create some kind of drug. I don't know what kind."

Cassidy had an idea. Flakka. DH-7's calling card, of sorts. Flakka was a designer synthetic street drug. It was a psychoactive mix of alpha-PVP, a cathinone, that made people act crazy—paranoid, delusional, agitated. Basically, they went crazy after taking it.

Cassidy had wanted answers. But part of her hadn't wanted this. She'd hoped Mae was wrong—dead wrong.

"I need to go," Mae said. "He's home. I'm trusting you with this information, Cady."

"I understand. Thank you for calling. I'm . . . praying for you."

"Don't stop. We need all the prayers we can get."

Cassidy hung up and turned to Ty. He stood behind her waiting, curious.

"What was that about?" he asked.

"Our plan worked."

CASSIDY AND TY sat at the dining room table, cups of reheated coffee in hand and some caramel corn spilling from a clear bag between them. Cassidy picked up a piece but didn't eat it. Not yet.

"When you were in Texas, I asked you to buy a track phone for me and to secure it under a Greyhound bus," Cassidy started.

He nodded. "Yes, you did. And I did. And you said you'd explain it all when I got back."

"That's right. I know a method of daisy-chaining the phones, so calls go to one phone and ping off it, while the actual call goes to another phone. It's confusing, but it works. It's a way of not being traced." Cassidy had learned about it in one of her investigations back in Seattle—a mob boss who'd been stealing money had utilized the trick.

"Okay. Go on."

She put her popcorn down, and her hands circled

her coffee mug instead. "Where was that Greyhound bus heading?"

"Florida." Realization swept over his face. "So that if that phone number does ping, the location would be all over the place."

"Exactly. I did it because I wanted to contact Lucy's family. I knew it was a risk. But I couldn't help but think Lucy's death was somehow connected with this whole mess. If I could figure that out, then maybe I could figure out what was going on with DH-7."

"Not sure if that was wise, but I'm following your logic."

Cassidy had expected he wouldn't approve. "After you did that—while you were gone—I called Lucy's father. He owns one of the top pharmaceutical companies in the world. He started as a chemist, and he's brilliant. I believe that DH-7 is coercing him somehow into developing new versions of flakka."

"That's not good. You called him? How did that go?"

"He was shocked to hear from me, to say the least. And then he panicked. He told me he had no idea what I was talking about. He hung up and refused to answer again. So I called Lucy's mom. She had a lot of the same reaction. But I could tell she knew more."

"And that was her that just called?"

Cassidy nodded, strains of their conversation replaying in her mind. "That's right. She pretty much confirmed what I'd begun to suspect. Lucy's father somehow got involved in the creation of flakka. Because of that, Lucy died. I believe he's still working with DH-7."

It sounded surreal to say the words out loud.

"Do you think Lucy's dad is the puppet master you've referred to before?"

"No, I think he's being blackmailed. Probably with Mae's life. She was the one who was supposed to die. After Lucy was murdered, Hiroto knew these guys weren't playing."

"This is becoming more twisted all the time, Cassidy." Ty grabbed her hand, squeezing it like he never wanted to let go.

"I know. And now I don't know what to do with this information. Ordinarily, I'd tell Samuel. But now he might be a bad guy, and Ryan is here claiming I should leave. I don't know who to go to with that information, who I can trust."

He leaned back and let out a thoughtful sigh. "There's no one above Ryan?"

"Ryan did mention that they'd brought someone in to fill Samuel's position. But I have no connection with this new guy. Besides, Ryan was just elected as prose-cuting attorney for the county. The only people above him would be on the federal level. I could go to the FBI, I suppose. But I don't have all the evidence concerning Lucy's murder. I just have hearsay and theories and a missing calendar page."

"You'll figure it out."

Cassidy took a sip of her coffee, but it wasn't as

satisfying as she'd hoped. Instead, she let her thoughts turn over and over again.

Ty's phone rang. He glanced at the number and squinted. "It's the Lantern Beach PD."

That was strange. Why were they calling Ty?

He put the phone to his ear and mumbled a few things before hanging up. "It's my cousin Ralph. Apparently, he decided to come into town to surprise me, but he was in a traffic accident."

"Is he okay?"

Ty nodded. "Yeah, but 'Redneck Dream' didn't fare as well. He needs someone to pick him up. I'll see if Austin can do it."

Cassidy hadn't met Ralph yet, but he'd named his obnoxious truck a title fitting for the vehicle. "Don't be silly. You can go pick him up."

Ty hesitated. "I don't know."

"I'll be fine."

"Leaving you isn't a good idea."

"I'll have Kujo and my gun," Cassidy said. "Besides, you'll be back in the blink of an eye."

Ty still didn't look convinced. "Are you sure about this?"

"I am. I'm going to drink my coffee and eat my caramel corn. Caramel corn makes everything better. At least, tonight it will."

True to her word, Cassidy sat at the table with her coffee and caramel corn. Her gun rested beside her, and Kujo sat at her feet. She passed the time slowly, not really scared but subdued over everything that had happened.

Outside, the wind was stirring up. The storm was getting closer, and darkness had fallen, making the change in atmosphere feel even more charged with danger.

It was going to take a while to comprehend the implications of today's events and news. Part of her still thought it might be a good idea to run. But who was she running from? Samuel? His henchmen?

She didn't know.

She popped another piece of caramel corn into her mouth. As she did, she heard something nearby.

Kujo did too—he barked, and his body went rigid, on alert.

Cassidy grabbed her gun, her throat feeling unnecessarily tight.

Had this Greg guy arranged that accident to get Ty out of the house? Was he here now for a moment of reckoning?

Before Cassidy could dive any further into the thought, she heard a cry.

A little kid's cry.

Her heart lurched at the sound. What was going on?

Footsteps—fast footsteps—raced up her stairs and pattered across her deck. More cries sounded. They were definitely coming from a child.

Throwing aside her promises, Cassidy rushed toward the noise. She threw the door open and froze.

A girl, probably twelve years old, stood there with tears streaming down her face. "Please, help!"

"What's wrong?" She placed her gun back on the table, trying not to scare the girl.

"My mom went for a swim. But she disappeared in the water. I can't find her. Please, help!"

Cassidy sucked in a breath. The undertow had been especially brutal lately. She'd seen uncountable rescues in the past couple of weeks. Many tourists didn't know any better than to go in the water anyway.

She shoved her phone into the girl's hand and locked the door behind her. "Call 911. Where's your mom?"

The girl pointed to the beach in front of Cassidy's place. "Right out there. You were the closest house. You've got to help her. Please."

"Kujo, stay," Cassidy ordered. She knew the dog would help comfort the girl.

Wasting no more time, Cassidy darted down her steps, across the dune, and toward the angry ocean.

Could she even save someone from rough surf like this? She didn't know. But she had to try.

She dove into the waves, immediately feeling the pressure of the water around her. The current tugged at her. Challenged her. Dared her to try and resist.

Cassidy came up for air, treading water. It was so dark out here. The water was so rough.

She swung her head around. She'd gotten farther

from shore than she'd thought. The undertow must be pulling her out—and fast.

Where was the girl's mother?

Cassidy glanced around again. She'd seen a head bobbing out here. Had the woman gone under? If so, where had she gone? How would Cassidy find the girl's mom?

On second thought, maybe Cassidy shouldn't have done this. She wasn't a strong enough swimmer. She glanced at the shore again.

She'd been swept out another several feet.

The current pulled at her. A wave splashed her face, going up her nose, making her cough.

Could she even make the swim back to shore?

Cassidy didn't know. It was like she'd been pulled by an unseen force—and a relentless one, at that.

Where was the girl? Had she called 911? Because they might need to do two rescues now.

No, Ty always told Cassidy not to panic. Panicking was the worst thing a person could do. She needed to swim horizontal to the current until she got out of it. Then she could swim back to shore.

If she wasn't too exhausted.

She *wouldn't* be. She could do this.

Why did Cassidy always want to be the hero? She should have just called 911 herself. But she'd seen that girl's face. Seen the panic. She had to help. She'd had no choice.

Another wave swept over her. She coughed, sputtering as water filled her mouth. No sooner did that wave pass over did another rise up. This one lifted her before cresting.

She looked at her house—a tiny light on the shoreline now.

She was getting farther and farther away.

Dear Lord, help me. Please. And help that girl's mother.

After uttering the prayer, Cassidy pulled herself together. She had to get out of this current. Giving up wasn't an option.

Using her last bit of energy, she began swimming horizontal to the shoreline. If she could just break the grip of the ocean, maybe she'd stand a chance.

Her arms already felt like gelatin, as did her legs. Cassidy was spent, and she knew it.

Cassidy paused a moment to rest and gather more energy. The waves continued to toss her. To lift and drop. Smother and push.

Darkness disoriented her. With every wave that crashed, the way back became more unclear.

She was going to get through this. She was going to rest a moment and then try again. And she'd keep trying until her feet hit that sandy shore near her house.

Then she'd have to tell that sweet little girl that she couldn't find her mother.

Cassidy could deal with that after she rescued herself, though. Dwelling on it now would only paralyze her.

She worked herself up, about to start swimming again.

But before she could, something brushed her ankle.

What was that? A shark?

Goosebumps pimpled her skin.

No, it didn't feel like a shark. Whatever it was squeezed her ankle.

And the next thing Cassidy knew, she was yanked under water.

TY PULLED into his driveway after dropping his cousin off at the campground where he was supposed to be staying. Yes, Ralph had arrived unexpectedly in town. He'd been planning on showing up on Ty's doorstep in the morning as a surprise—until he'd gotten run off the road right after he left the ferry. His truck would now need some major repair work.

Ralph and his truck weren't Ty's biggest concern right now. Right now, he wanted to get back to Cassidy.

He started to walk up to Cassidy's door when his phone buzzed. It was a text message from Cassidy.

I'm sorry.

His pulse spiked. She was sorry? For what?
Ty typed back:

What does that mean?

He paused outside her cottage door, anxiety overtaking his muscles. Something was wrong. Really wrong. Kujo barked inside—a frantic kind of bark. Ty tried the door, but it was locked.

I couldn't bear to tell you goodbye. But I've left. It's the right thing to do.

Cassidy had left? What? Why would she do that? They'd talked about this.

Yet he knew Cassidy just might take things into her own hands, especially if it meant protecting the people she loved. He couldn't let her do that.

Where'd you go?

Her car was still in the driveway, as was her ice cream truck. How did she leave? With Ryan?

I can't tell you. I need to stay hidden until the trial. It's the only way.

A surge of anger burned inside Ty. How could Cassidy do this? He resisted the urge to punch the wall. It would do no good.

He should have never left. Had Cassidy been waiting for Ty to leave so she could make her getaway?

He took a deep breath. He had to calm down.

Ty had a spare key to Cassidy's place, and he jammed it into the lock. Stepping inside her house, he glanced around. Everything appeared normal, with no signs of distress. But why had she left her gun on the table? Wouldn't she take it with her?

A moment of loss swept over him.

Cassidy really was gone.

As if reading Ty's thoughts, Kujo whined beside him.

Would she come back? Or was this the end for them?

Ty couldn't let himself believe that.

Cassidy loved him. He'd seen it in her eyes.

Things weren't going to end like this.

If Cassidy was leaving Lantern Beach, she would have to take the ferry. It was the only way off the island since there were no bridges.

Ty rushed to his truck. With any luck, he could catch Cassidy before she left.

Cassidy awoke to blackness.

Total dark without a smidgen of light.

Where was she? What had happened?

She could hardly breathe. Hardly move. Not with the questions pressing on her.

That was when she heard a rumble. Felt bumps.

She reached for her face but couldn't move her arms. She jerked them again.

They were bound behind her.

She kicked her legs.

They were bound as well.

A blindfold. That must be why she couldn't see.

At least, she wasn't gagged too.

The events of tonight rushed back to her.

She'd tried to save that woman from drowning. But that woman had never really been out in the ocean, had she? And that little girl . . . she'd lied. Someone had put her up to this somehow. It had all been a trap.

Another swimmer—a stronger one—had been in those waters, waiting for just the right moment to tug Cassidy under. She must have passed out.

Maybe there'd been a boat nearby. Maybe someone had pulled her inside.

She wasn't sure what had happened after that. She couldn't remember anything.

Only now. This moment.

Cassidy jerked against her restraints again. It was no use. They were too tight. And she couldn't see to be able to find any tools to help her.

Maybe she could feel around.

She moved her hands again, and rough carpet embedded with wood splinters and dried leaves scratched her skin.

A car. She was in the trunk of a car, wasn't she? That would explain the bumps. The white noise of the tires rotating against the road.

Cassidy scooted back and felt around the perimeter of the space. But it was no use. The trunk was empty, with only Cassidy inside.

Who had snatched her? Greg? Samuel? Where was this person taking her?

And even worse: what would he do with Cassidy when they got there?

And then the sounds stopped.

The car wasn't moving anymore.

Cassidy braced herself for whatever was to come.

CHAPTER
TEN

TY RACED TOWARD THE FERRY, desperate to find Cassidy. He'd seen Ryan's car before and knew it was a dark-blue sedan with rental stickers on the back. If only he could locate it . . . maybe he could stop Cassidy from leaving. Ty could convince her they could do this together.

Or would Ty be wiser just to let her go? To make her own choices?

He frowned, and his grip tightened on the steering wheel.

He wasn't sure what the right answer was. He only knew he was going to fight for the two of them. He wasn't giving up this easily.

Ten minutes later, Ty reached the docks. As he pulled into the loading area, his stomach twisted, and he hit his hand against the steering wheel.

The last boat of the night glided across the dark water.

Ty was five minutes too late.

Five minutes.

He closed his eyes.

Lord, what now?

Only one thought slammed into his mind.

Don't give up.

That was right. He wasn't going to give up. There was a chance Cassidy wasn't even on that ferry.

He threw his truck in park, climbed out, and jogged toward the attendant standing near the entrance of the loading dock. The man's eyes narrowed before flashing with recognition.

"I remember you," the man said. "You and your girlfriend helped get that bomb off the ferry back in August."

Perfect. The man already felt some goodwill toward him. "That was me."

"You were a real lifesaver that day. Could have turned out a lot uglier."

"You're right. I'm thankful it worked out like it did." Ty paused. "Listen, I need a favor. Did you, by chance, see a dark-blue sedan board just now?"

The attendant glanced at his clipboard and shrugged. "I can't say I pay that much attention or have that good of a memory. Sorry."

The man obviously wasn't taking this seriously enough. Ty had to get through to him. "It's really important. If you could just try to remember . . ."

The man drummed his fingers against the clipboard

and looked off into the distance at the lights of the ferry. "I have to be honest. I see hundreds of cars come through here each day. It's been especially busy this week with the fishing tournament."

"There was no car matching that description? No one acting suspiciously?"

"I'm sorry. I wish I could help. There's security camera footage, but it's going to be hard to see much other than license plates since it's so dark out here."

Ty took a step back. He knew the man didn't have anything else to offer. Talking to him was a dead end. "I understand. Thanks."

He might be leaving the docks, but this wasn't over. Ty just had to figure out his next steps.

Cassidy waited on the scratchy carpet lining the car's trunk, anticipating what might happen next.

She couldn't stand the fact that she couldn't see anything. That she couldn't defend herself. That she was at someone else's mercy.

Her wet clothes were beginning to dry, and they smelled like seawater. Strands of her hair clung to her face. Occasionally, she coughed, and water from her lungs began to rattle in her chest.

What about Ty? Had he returned from helping Ralph yet? Had he discovered she was gone? Would he look for her?

Or had whoever was behind this planned all of that also? Had they hurt Ty? Had they orchestrated the accident Ty's cousin was in?

Cassidy's heart ached at the thought of it.

Please Lord, let him be okay. Don't let him get hurt because of me.

She'd already searched the trunk to the best of her ability three different times. She'd hoped to find a wrench or a jack or some kind of tool.

There was nothing.

So she waited some more.

Nothing was happening.

Finally, a door opened and then slammed shut.

Footsteps sounded. But they faded.

The driver wasn't coming to get Cassidy. He was walking away.

Was this guy just going to leave her here to die?

The thought caused a surge of panic to rise in Cassidy.

Someone could leave her here, trapped in the back of this car and unable to get out. It wouldn't take long for her body to succumb to the ravages of dehydration and lack of food.

Then Cassidy couldn't testify. She'd be no good at the trial. In fact, DH-7 leaders might walk free.

Especially since Samuel had the evidence needed to put them away.

Sure, Cassidy had a copy of it. But she hadn't told anyone where she put it.

Not even Ty.

Ty gripped his phone. He'd called Mac and told him about Cassidy's texts and her supposed plan to leave.

"I'll be on the lookout," Mac promised. "I know this isn't what you want to hear, but maybe you should let Cassidy do what she thinks is best."

Ty was fully willing to do that. He just didn't think that Cassidy leaving was truly the best thing.

"Thanks, Mac. Believe me, I'm trying to think through all of the options."

"I know you are," Mac said. "I'll be in touch if I hear anything."

Ty pulled to a stop at the only inn in town and scanned the parking lot. He didn't see any sedans matching Ryan's. He needed to confirm if Ryan was here or not.

After trying to shrug off some of his visible tension, Ty stepped inside and smiled at the woman at the front desk. She put her book down—a romance with a shirtless military man on the front—and her cheeks reddened when she looked up at Ty.

She cleared her throat before asking, "How can I help you?"

"I'm looking for someone, and I don't know if he's checked out yet or not."

"I can't share that information." She offered a tight

smile, as if awkward about her firm stance. Or maybe it was Ty's presence that had her acting strangely.

"It's important."

She shrugged. "That's what people always say."

"Life or death."

"Do you have a warrant?"

Okay, Ty needed to try a different approach here. "I'm afraid my girlfriend is in danger."

The woman studied him a moment before averting her gaze. "You're that former Navy SEAL, aren't you?"

He nodded, hoping that fact might work in his favor. "I am."

She remained silent a moment before hunching up her shoulders and letting out a sigh. "Did you tell the police?"

"I just got off the phone with the chief. I really need to know if someone has checked out yet. You would be my hero if you helped me out here."

Her cheeks turned pink again. "You're going to get me in trouble."

"I won't tell anyone."

She stayed quiet a moment and then let out a sigh. "What's his name?"

"Ryan Samson."

Her eyes brightened. "Oh, Mr. Samson. He's a nice man. As far as I know, he's still here. Said he was staying until tomorrow."

"Has anything stood out about him?" Ty knew he was pushing his luck, but he needed to find out as much as he could.

"He's on the phone a lot. I don't know if that helps, though."

Just then, the door opened, and Ryan walked in.

Jackpot.

But if Ryan was still here, did that mean Cassidy had left alone? And, if so, how had she done that without a car?

CASSIDY FELT certain she'd been in this trunk for hours. Just like she felt certain she would die here.

Alone.

How appropriate that the girl who'd prided herself in being independent would have no one there in her final moments.

She shook her head, trying to snap herself from her thoughts.

No, that was the old Cassidy—or, should she say, Cady? She'd found her niche here. She had friends. Love. A church.

She was no longer a lone ranger. A poor little rich girl. A woman living for herself.

Cassidy coughed again, more water aspirating from her lungs.

She could have died out there in the ocean. She shivered at the thought. It almost seemed preferable to dying in here now.

All she remembered was going under. Being certain death was near. But Greg or whoever targeted her must have grabbed her. Pulled her into a boat maybe. Revived her before she died. Had he drugged her also?

It was a possibility.

"Help me!" Cassidy yelled again.

But there was no response—just as there hadn't been any response when she'd screamed earlier.

Why were there no noises around Cassidy now? It was totally silent. No waves. No other cars. No crickets or frogs even.

Where was she exactly?

Had Samuel orchestrated this? It was the only thing that made sense. Had he sent someone to abduct her?

But Cassidy never got that sense of threat from Samuel. She'd always felt she could trust him.

And that was what made all of this even harder.

She couldn't just lie here and die.

It went against every instinct in her. Certainly there had to be a way she could get out of this car—even if she was blindfolded and bound.

Carefully, she scooted until she hit the back of the trunk. More carpet scratched her fingertips. She'd already checked everything within reach in this trunk.

Now it was time to check things that were out of her reach.

Most modern cars had some kind of lever people could pull if stuck in the trunk—if Cassidy could find it. She'd be feeling blindly again, but it was worth a try. It beat roasting in here.

Sweat already covered her skin. Soaked her clothes. Or was that the seawater still? She wasn't sure.

It didn't matter.

She lifted herself up on her knees and managed to turn so her arms faced the latch area—she thought.

Where was the button that would release the trunk?

She couldn't reach high enough lying on her side like this.

She managed to arch her back and prop herself up on her knees for just long enough to feel up higher along the edge of the trunk.

Her fingers connected with something . . . different. A hard plastic? Was this it?

Still angled into a position that made it hard to breathe, she managed to stay that way long enough to wrap her fingers beneath the lever.

Cassidy tugged.

Heard a pop.

And fresh air swept through the trunk.

She'd done it! She'd opened the trunk.

Now she just needed to get out and find help.

A cry wanted to escape from deep within her. With her binds and blindfold, it would be hard to escape. Nearly impossible.

But she'd seen the impossible happen before.

She threw her legs out of the trunk and inched her body forward. She needed to use her body weight to leverage her escape. Finally, the balance tilted, and her body rocked forward. Her feet connected with something soft. Grass, if Cassidy had to guess.

She drew herself upright and tried to find her equilibrium.

This was the tricky part.

Maybe if she could find some woods. Find a stick there to help cut her binds. Find a tree to hide behind.

Yet she couldn't see anything. She'd already tried to rub the blindfold off, but it hadn't worked. The cloth was too tight.

She hopped forward a step when she felt something on her arm.

Something *grasping* her arm.

"I was curious to see how long that would take you, Ms. Matthews," a deep voice said. "Well done. Well done."

Ty stood in the lobby area of the inn and stared at Ryan Samson. At his neatly pressed clothes. His immovable hair. His confused expression.

Ryan mirrored his look, looking equally surprised to see Ty there. His hands went to his hips, and his eyes narrowed.

"Ty." Ryan's voice sounded icy cool. "What are you doing here?"

Ty got right to the point. "Have you heard from Cassidy?"

Ryan's face remained masked and expressionless. "Not since earlier. Why?"

"I got a text from her saying that she left." The words still caused a bitter taste in Ty's mouth.

The mask slipped, and Ryan's eyebrows pushed together. "What do you mean by *left*?"

"I mean, she thought it was best if she got out of town. Yet you're still here."

"She didn't talk to me," Ryan said.

"So you have no idea where she is?" Ty still wasn't sure he bought it.

"I have no clue."

Ty released his breath and turned away from the man. His thoughts barreled through his mind like a runaway freight train.

"You think she was taken?" Ryan asked.

"I do." As Ty said the words, another thought hit him. He needed to talk to Ralph again. He pulled out his phone and dialed his number.

Ralph answered on the first ring. "What's up, Ty?"

"Ralph, did you tell anyone you were coming here?"

"I guess you could say that. I put it on Facebook. Figured you never checked it, so it didn't make a difference."

"So anyone who went to your page could have seen it?"

"I guess. Why?"

"Just wondering. Thanks." Ty hung up, and the truth washed over him.

That accident hadn't been a mistake. No, someone had wanted Ty to get out of the house, to leave Cassidy. And Ralph had offered the perfect excuse.

"I'm going to look for her." Ty started toward the door.

Ryan followed behind him. "I'll help."

"I'm not sure that's a good idea."

Ryan grabbed his arm, and Ty stopped in his tracks. "Why wouldn't it be?"

"Because how do we know we can even trust you? You waltz back in here and that same day she disappears?" Anger crept into Ty's words. Things weren't adding up, and Ty couldn't shake the thought that Ryan was somehow involved.

"If I was the bad guy and I'd shot at her, I wouldn't have missed."

"Do you have any idea who was behind that?"

"Samuel, if I had to guess. Maybe he wanted her off the island so he could attack. When that didn't work, he moved on to Plan B."

"An FBI agent with aim that bad? It's suspicious, to say the least."

Ryan stared back, his eyes blazing. "Listen, I came here to protect Cassidy. I came here because I knew if I could find her, others could. And I heard about the gunshot down at the boardwalk today. Do you think that's a coincidence?"

"I don't know what to think anymore."

"Well, if someone did take her, it wasn't me. I'm here. Besides, my bets are on Samuel."

Ty didn't say anything.

"We can stand here and argue for the rest of the

night, or we can get out there and look for her," Ryan said. "I know which one I'm in favor of."

Ty still wasn't sure if he trusted the man or not, but standing here wasn't doing any good. "You're right. Let's go."

"I'm going to call some people to help," Ty said. "And then I'm going to take this island street by street."

CASSIDY FROZE ON THE GRASS. The man squeezed her arm so tightly she nearly yelped. Now that she was out of the car's trunk, she could smell the scent of sea air.

Somewhere in the far distance, she thought she heard a car. Maybe she wasn't as far removed from civilization as she'd thought. The sounds had just been muffled.

The man's voice came back to her. He sounded strangely familiar, yet she couldn't pinpoint where she'd heard him before. Still, she knew who her abductor most likely was.

She licked her lips. "You're Greg, aren't you?"

"I presumed you'd be smart enough to figure that out."

"Samuel sent you?" She desperately wished she had her vision, that she could take in her surroundings. Though she assumed she was still on Lantern Beach, what if she wasn't? Greg could have taken her somewhere else.

Not knowing made her feel disoriented and off-balance.

"You ask too many questions," he growled.

"I only asked one."

He jerked her, and Cassidy lurched forward, nearly stumbling to the ground. She struggled to remain upright as he dragged her away. Her bound legs couldn't keep up.

"We'll have plenty of time to talk," Greg assured her, a hint of amusement in his voice. He was enjoying this.

The air left her lungs. Getting enjoyment out of the suffering of others? That was never a good thing.

"You were the one who shot at me earlier, weren't you?"

"Smart girl."

"You missed. On purpose."

"I was trying to get you away from your friends and off this island. Thought it would be easier. But it became apparent that wasn't going to work."

"So you lured me out to the beach and tried to drown me?"

"That's right. I knew you couldn't turn down helping a poor girl whose mom was drowning."

"Why not just let me die?"

"Because I have other plans for you."

Cassidy's lungs froze until she could hardly breathe. This man was desperate to hurt her. And he was going to do just that unless she stopped him.

"Where are you taking me?" Her words came out in rasps as she slid along the ground behind Greg.

"Somewhere secluded, where no one will hear you if you scream."

Her blood frosted as fear ricocheted through her.

This was it. This was the moment she'd been dreading.

Cassidy had known from the start of her assignment with DH-7 how things might end. She'd just prayed those were only worst-case scenarios. Now they all seemed to be coming to fruition—to her detriment.

She didn't want to go anywhere with this man. Because anywhere she went would certainly lead to death.

Using a burst of strength, Cassidy jerked out of the man's grasp and swung around. Without her feet or hands—or even sight—there wasn't but so much she could do.

But she could use her head.

Literally.

Before she could second-guess herself, Cassidy charged toward him.

A click stopped her cold.

The click of a gun being cocked.

"I have my Glock aimed at you." Greg's voice sounded cool enough to cause a new rush of nerves in Cassidy. "If you try anything, I'll shoot your shoulder. Then your knee. And anywhere else I want that won't kill you. You'll slowly bleed out. Do you understand?"

She cringed, believing every word he said—without a doubt. "Yeah, I hear you."

"Good. Then move." He shoved her again.

This time, Cassidy hit the ground, unable to catch herself. Her shoulder ached on impact, and even her teeth felt jarred.

Greg grabbed her arm and pulled her upright again. He didn't let go this time—his grip was vise-like—as he dragged her up two steps and into a building.

A house, maybe?

Once inside, he shoved Cassidy into a chair, wrapped a rope around her midsection, and then tugged off her blindfold.

Slowly, things came into focus.

A small cottage.

Old, outdated furniture.

Everything covered in dust.

Only a candle to light the space.

And Greg stood there with a gun in his hand. The man matched the one Cassidy had seen on that surveillance video—except he was shorter than she'd anticipated. But his height didn't make him any less scary. His arms were muscular, his neck thick, and his eyes contained the wrong kind of focus—the deadly kind.

He wore black, military-style pants with a white T-shirt that hugged his toned chest.

When the whole picture came together, Cassidy realized one thing: this man was no joke. And she felt certain she'd seen him somewhere before. She just wasn't certain where that place was.

Her gaze traveled beside him. A table of sharp, shiny objects waited there.

Cassidy's pulse surged as she realized the truth.

Torture devices.

This would be her worst nightmare coming true.

"Now, let's not waste any more time." Greg turned to her with a gleam in his eyes. "Where did you hide the information?"

Ty had hit nearly every street on the island—twice.

The problem was he didn't know what he was looking for. But he was pretty sure he hadn't found it.

As his frustration mounted, he pulled his car to the side of the road to gather his thoughts. It had already been two hours—two long hours of searching with no answers. Darkness had long since descended over the island, and people had begun to settle down for the night.

But for Ty, this night was just starting.

He was ready to go door-to-door, but even doing that, he wasn't sure how far he'd get. It seemed futile, like it would take too much time without enough payoff.

If Cassidy was still on the island, her captor wouldn't readily give up information. Wouldn't easily share that she might be held captive in one of the houses here. And that made all of this feel like a wild goose chase.

What if Cassidy wasn't here? What if no one had taken her? What if, as her texts suggested, she'd left on her own?

Ty couldn't believe it—*wouldn't* believe it.

Mac was trying to trace the location of Cassidy's phone, but it was taking time. Ryan was supposedly hitting the streets and talking to people as well. Maybe his big-city charm would win people over and he'd find answers—though Ty doubted it.

But it was now almost midnight. With every minute Cassidy was gone, the likelihood she wouldn't return increased.

Ty leaned toward the steering wheel as he tried to get some deep breaths.

He needed to think this through. What was he missing?

Think, Ty. Think.

Where would Cassidy be? What was the best way to find her?

He closed his eyes. What would he have done as a SEAL to locate a missing person? He'd use every resource at his disposal—satellite imagery, word of mouth, surveillance video. He'd trace the person's last steps. Look at any evidence left behind.

Ty didn't exactly have satellites here, but there were security cameras on some of the local businesses. He could talk to people. Maybe someone had seen something.

Those were really his only options right now.

Just then, his phone rang. Mac's number popped on the screen.

Maybe the interim police chief had better news.

"What's going on?" Ty asked.

"We just had a woman come into the police station. Said a man bribed her daughter. Said she could audition for a new reality show. All she had to do was go up to another cast member and convince this woman that her mom was drowning in the ocean."

"Cassidy?" His heart beat out of control.

"You know it."

That just confirmed what Ty already thought: Cassidy hadn't left the island. No, someone had done something to her.

ORION KEPT his vise-like grip on Cady's arm as they walked down the street, and Tyron remained behind them, his presence menacing and ensuring there wouldn't be any funny business.

It was dark outside—scary dark. At one time, there had been overhead streetlights, but delinquents had thrown rocks at them and busted the bulbs. The darkness helped conceal their escapades—helped to conceal them—while it made other people victims.

"You have no idea what's going on?" Cady tried to pull out of Orion's grip, but it was no use. "You're probably going to make me lose my job, you know."

"I'm just doing what I've been told. I heard we have a narc."

Her blood felt icy enough to cause heart failure. "Is that right? Who would be that stupid?"

"No idea. I think Raul wants to root that person out."

Why hadn't Cady just run? Not even gone into the drugstore? She should have kept walking and feigned an excuse. Instead, she'd fallen back on logic and reasoning. She should have trusted her instinct instead.

"I wonder how he plans to do that."

"I heard it's going to be heart-wrenching, whatever it is."

What did that even mean? Did she want to know? And why wouldn't Orion let go of her?

Sweat scattered across her forehead and skin. Her skin felt burning hot, yet her insides felt like they'd frozen. The mix had been like two fronts colliding inside her, creating the storm of the century.

She and Orion were the last ones to arrive back at the compound. Everyone else had gathered in a large space on the bottom level, one that had been used as a laundry area at one time. Now it was just cement walls that were stained with unimaginable things.

Cady's stomach turned when she stepped into the doorway and everyone turned to stare.

Don't go in. Don't go in.

But as much as her internal voice warned her to stay away, she knew she couldn't turn back. The instant she did, everyone would know she was guilty. She was the traitor. The rat.

"Now that we're all here, I have something to talk to you about," Raul said. Tattoos stretched across his skin —nearly every visible inch of it. The man's eyes were dark—so dark they reminded Cady of black holes— empty yet deadly. He was tall with thick muscles.

Everyone had formed a loose circle around him, and he began to pace the perimeter. The gang's full attention was on their infamous leader—someone who not only was street smart, but who had more business sense than the leaders of most of the start-up companies here in Seattle.

Cady had underestimated him.

And that had been her first mistake.

Raul grimaced as he stared each member in the face. Only the people he trusted were allowed here. The rest of the gang members were spread out across the West Coast. They did Raul's dirty work and were minions in his quest for dominance.

His need for power and control was unlike anything Cady had ever seen. It was like a virus that consumed everything in its path—a virus that was nearly at epidemic levels.

"My men found a traitor. They didn't give me a name. Not yet. So I told them to do what they needed to do." He paused and held something up. "And they did."

Cady squinted, trying to see what was in his hand. It was a photo of . . . something.

It was red. And messy.

Part of her didn't want to know.

Yet she couldn't unglue her eyes.

She *had* to know.

Raul walked closer, holding out the photo so everyone could see it better. When he circled near her, her stomach dropped like an elevator whose cables had snapped.

That was an organ. A . . . heart?

"That's right. This is what happens to traitors. They rip my heart out. So you know what I do to them? I rip their hearts out too."

His guys had literally taken out someone's heart?

Cady could hardly breathe.

What kind of vile people were these? Did they not give a second thought to the sanctity of life?

She knew the answer.

No, they didn't.

"We have another traitor in our midst." Raul started to pace again. "And I'm going to figure out who it is. And you'll be treated the same way that you've treated me. You knew from the start that I demand loyalty. And, in return, I provide for you. You all have a good life here. Nothing makes me more disgusted than this."

The air in the room changed. Everyone was scared—even those who were loyal. Cady could feel it.

While, on one hand, these people would take another life without batting an eyelash, on the other hand, they feared dying. Did anyone else see the irony? Probably not.

"We're going to figure out who you are," Raul said.

"How do you know there is someone?" another member asked before pounding his fist against his chest. "I'd never betray you."

"Some information has come to light recently. That's all I need to say."

Cady tried to keep her face expressionless. No one

knew she'd copied some files from Raul's computer. That she was the one who would betray him. That she was the narc.

"Now we're going to have some one-on-one talks," Raul continued. "And we're going to figure this out. No one is leaving until we do."

TODAY'S GOALS: SURVIVE.

WHERE DID *you hide the information?*

The question echoed in Cassidy's mind as she stared at Greg. Her jaw throbbed. Her shoulder hurt. She continued to cough up water.

And now this headache. What information was he talking about? The jump drive Samuel had sent her? That didn't make sense. What if Greg thought she had other evidence? Was that what this was about?

"I don't know what information you're talking about," she finally said.

She glanced at Greg's watch as he paced in front of her.

It was already well past midnight. A new day.

It had been three hours since she disappeared.

Was Ty out looking for her? Would he ever find her? Or would it all end here without so much as a goodbye?

The thought clogged her throat.

"Of course you know what the information is." Greg paced in front of her, the gun still in his hands.

Fear seemed to crackle in the air, filling the space like a gas leak. And, just like the aforementioned leak, one spark—one mistake—could ignite the world around her in an explosion she couldn't escape from.

Cassidy tugged against her restraints, but it was no use. She couldn't move. Greg had tied her tightly to the chair, and she'd be hard pressed to get away.

"No, really—I don't. Are you talking about the jump drive that I turned in to the FBI?"

Did they suspect she'd kept part of it? Was that what this was about?

"We know you have a copy of it," Greg said. "And we want it."

She needed to buy time. "Why would I save a copy of it?"

"Stop playing stupid." He slapped his hand across her cheek.

The breath left Cassidy's lungs as the stinging on her face jarred her thoughts. One hit like that wasn't going to stop her. Not yet.

"You searched my cottage earlier, didn't you?" She hadn't been going crazy when she'd thought her magazines and various papers had been straightened.

"Yes, I did." A smug grin tugged at his lips.

"But you didn't find anything. Because there isn't anything. I turned it all over to Samuel."

His grin disappeared. "You're clever. You're too

smart to leave anything out in the open, but that doesn't mean there's nothing there."

Cassidy watched the man as he paced. She'd guess he was contemplating his options, trying to figure out what to do with Cassidy next.

"What are you going to do to me?" she finally asked.

"Make sure you're not alive to testify at the trial, of course."

She'd known that was the end game, hadn't she? If she shared what she knew, she died. If she didn't share, she died. So why give them what they wanted anyway? "Then just get it over with. Kill me now."

"Not until I have what I want."

"Why's it so important to you anyway?" She stared at him. He seemed tightly wound, like a toy soldier thoughtlessly doing his job—a toy that might malfunction at any minute. When that happened, the outcome could be in Cassidy's favor or his.

She wasn't sure she wanted to find out.

Greg leaned closer. "If you hid those documents, they could change the face of the trial. We can't have that happening."

Cassidy studied him. That was the second time he'd used "we." Of course he was working with someone. How many people were in on this? "You and Samuel are in this together?"

He scowled. "That's none of your business."

"You must be really loyal to come all the way out here and do his dirty work."

He turned away from her and picked up something

from the tray. A scalpel. He began examining the sharp tip. "You're not helping yourself right now."

"I'm just trying to figure out what makes you tick. What would motivate a man to give up everything to come out here and demand information that probably won't affect him either way. It's either loyalty—misplaced at best—or money." Cassidy stared at him, stared at the instrument in his hand. She tried to ignore it, to stay focused. But she was having a hard time. "I'm guessing money right now."

"Shut up!" He turned toward her, his eyes blazing.

Cassidy pulled back, afraid he might slap her again.

But he only stared, venom oozing from every part of him.

The next instant, he thrust the scalpel to her throat. "Where is it?"

She dared not breathe for fear of being pricked. "I honestly . . . don't know . . . what you're . . . talking about."

One wrong move and the sharp blade would cut her. She could slowly bleed out.

Wait . . . what if it was the information that Samuel had sent her? Was that what Greg wanted? But . . . if he worked for Samuel, what sense did that make?

It *didn't* make any sense.

Samuel would have that information.

So would Ryan.

So who else was behind this?

Or was the information Greg sought something totally different?

Ty paced across the floor of Mac's office at the police station. They'd met back here to discuss things and to set up a base of operations. Ty's inner circle—Austin, Wes, Skye, and Lisa—had been called in to help and were now searching the streets.

Meanwhile, Mac had talked to officials, persuading them to check the vehicles leaving the ferry in Hatteras. If Cassidy was on that boat, hopefully someone would find her.

Quinton had gone to the marina to see if anyone there had seen someone matching Cassidy's description.

They were trying to cover all their bases. But, for a small island, the town was feeling really big right now.

Mac strode back into the room. He'd been questioning the woman who came in, who claimed her daughter had been manipulated to lure Cassidy out of the house.

Ty stopped pacing, anxious to hear his update.

"The man who bribed that girl fits the description of the person who came into the police station and asked about Cassidy," Mac said.

"So it's Greg, Samuel's right-hand man."

"That's our best guess at this point. This man—Greg—drew Cassidy out, knowing she wouldn't be able to stop herself from helping a frantic little girl whose mother was in trouble. He must have grabbed Cassidy when she was trying to help and taken her somewhere."

What had Cassidy gone through? What was she going through now? Ty could hardly handle the thoughts.

"Greg most likely had enough time to get to the ferry." Ty didn't want the words to leave his lips, but they did. Because they were true. And if Greg was on the ferry, then, at this point, he and Cassidy could be anywhere.

"We're trying to confirm that."

"I suppose it's a possibility also that there was a boat waiting somewhere. We should probably check at the docks."

"Of course." Mac paused. "And I know you don't want to hear this, but I also called in the Coast Guard. They're searching the waters . . . just in case."

Ty sucked in a breath. He knew just what Mac was saying. Just in case Cassidy had drowned out there while trying to rescue someone who wasn't drowning.

An ache formed in his chest.

Mac's radio crackled.

"Chief, we've got a car here at the General Store." Quinton's voice came on over the speaker, static breaking in. "You're going to want to see it."

"I'm on my way." Mac put his radio back on his belt and motioned to Ty. "Come on. You're going with me."

They hopped in his police cruiser and headed down the island's main road. As the minutes seemed to crawl past, Ty braced himself for whatever they might find.

They stopped a few minutes later in the parking lot of the local convenience store.

Normally at this time of night—two a.m.—the streets were quiet. It wasn't a nightlife kind of community. But right now the store was a hotbed of activity.

Quinton's police car was in the lot, lights blazing. One other vehicle was near the front of the store. An employee, if Ty had to guess.

The building was nothing to write home about, so to speak. It was a simple one-story structure with a white brick veneer. The sign at the top read Swanner's Market in patriotic red, white, and blue letters. It was a great location to grab overpriced supplies or to get gas when in a pinch.

He followed Mac toward the back of the building, stopping in an overflow parking area near the dumpster. Quinton waited there beside a car.

The officer looked a little paler than usual—actually, he looked like he could throw up.

"There's blood inside," Quinton started. "The door was open. That's why someone called it in. They came out to make sure everything was okay. That's when they saw the . . . red stuff. It's on the front seat, and there's a lot of it."

Ty stared at the car—a sedan.

Rental company information was on the back windshield.

He sucked in a breath.

It was Ryan's.

"I NEED you to come with me for a minute." Greg used the scalpel to cut through a section of rope behind Cassidy. Her binds fell to the floor.

Greg put down the scalpel, grabbed Cassidy's arm, and pulled her from the chair.

Her temporary relief was quickly replaced with a new round of anxiety. "Where are you taking me?"

"None of your business."

Worst-case scenarios rushed through her mind. She wanted to argue. To try and stop him. But she had no time.

He opened a door across the room and shoved her inside. She tumbled into a sea of old dusty coats before landing against a canister vacuum cleaner. An old closet, she realized.

The door slammed, and Cassidy heard something sliding across the floor.

Greg was making sure she didn't get out. If she had

to guess, he'd shoved some furniture in front of it. Why in the world would he stop to put her in here?

Cassidy listened carefully. Heard his footsteps fading. Heard a door open. Then shut.

Then silence.

He'd left, hadn't he? Why?

Cassidy mulled over what she'd learned—or what she *hadn't* learned. She really knew nothing more. She only had more questions. What exactly was this information he'd mentioned? What Samuel had sent, or something else? What was Samuel's role in this? Ryan's?

The questions overwhelmed her.

But this was no time to sit on her hands. There had to be something in here to help her get out.

Leveraging herself against the wall, Cassidy managed to stand. Metal coat hangers clanged together above her.

Perfect.

Using her chin, she knocked one to the floor. Then Cassidy lowered herself again and carefully found the hanger with her bound hands. She began working the edge against the duct tape around her wrists.

Come on. Work. Please work!

She methodically moved the metal point against the tape. Again and again. Over and over.

Finally, she heard a rip.

It was working!

A few more scrapes later, and the binds broke.

Her heart sputtered with relief.

Wasting no time, she scratched the binds at her ankles until the tape there split also.

She stood—the best she could in the cramped closet. Then she pushed on the door.

It didn't budge.

Whatever Greg had shoved in front of it was heavy enough that Cassidy couldn't move it out of the way.

She leaned her forehead against the smooth wood of the door and let her thoughts run wild. Her heart drummed in her ears like a battle cry, each thrum increasing her anxiety and solidifying her realizations.

Cassidy had only one choice. She had to defend herself when Greg returned.

She felt her way around the closet. Felt the vacuum. Felt coats—with nothing in their pockets. Felt some movies on the top shelf.

She found the only thing that might possibly work as a weapon.

A DVD.

She cracked it in half, revealing a sharp, jagged edge. Then she gripped the broken disc in her hands, ready to use it like a knife.

And it was just in time.

She heard a door open.

Footsteps sounded.

Furniture moved.

Cassidy stood on guard, ready to pounce.

But when the door opened, Greg stood there with a gun to Ryan's head.

"One wrong move, and he dies," Greg said.

Ty squatted beside the seat and touched the liquid on the car seat—the seat where Ryan had most likely been sitting only moments ago.

"The blood is still warm," Ty said. "That means that whatever happened, it was recent."

Mac nodded, grim lines across his face. "You're right. And if it happened recently, that might mean that Cassidy is still on the island."

"That's the one bit of good news, I suppose. We've got to figure out how to find her." Ty took a napkin Mac offered him and wiped his fingers.

"I'll see if I can find some security camera footage from here at the store and talk to the owner. I'll get Quinton to check other businesses in the area."

"I'll look through the car," Ty said. "If you don't mind me interfering with your investigation."

He said it to be polite. They both knew Ty was going to investigate with permission or without.

"Please do. Consider yourself deputized, just for today. I need all the help I can get."

Ty wasted no time. He climbed into the other side of the car and opened the glove box. It only had the normal items—the car's owner manual, a tire pressure gauge, a small first aid kit.

Turning on the light on his phone, he swept the rest of the vehicle, looking for any kind of clue.

Something glimmered between the front seats. Ty

reached between into the space and pulled out a cell phone.

Ryan's cell phone, most likely. He must have dropped it when he was injured or abducted.

He clicked on the screen. It was passcode protected.

Of course.

Ty slapped a mosquito on his neck as he thought about what to do.

What would Ryan's code be? Ty didn't know him well enough to take many guesses. On impulse, he typed in Cassidy's birthday. The phone vibrated, telling him he was wrong.

Two more chances.

He had no idea what else Ryan might use for his code.

Ty paused, thinking things through.

He heard once on how to hack someone's phone. Strangely enough, his cousin Ralph had told him about the idea. It seemed worth giving a try since Ty didn't have any other options.

He clicked on the phone's virtual assistant and asked for the time. When the numbers came on the screen, Ty clicked on them, which brought him to the Clock app on the phone.

Ty's pulse pounded harder. Would this actually work?

It seemed like a possibility.

What had Ralph told him to do next? He closed his eyes, trying to remember that conversation—one that had seemed so inconsequential at the time.

Once on the Clock app, Ty found a button to buy more ringtones. That took him to the app store.

And that allowed him to get inside Ryan's phone.

It worked. He couldn't believe it, but he wasn't complaining right now.

Wasting no more time, he scrolled through Ryan's phone log. There were several calls made today to the same number. It had a Seattle area code.

Interesting.

Ty did a reverse number lookup, but the number was unlisted. Not surprising.

He moved on to Ryan's text messages. A lot were from his work. One was from a woman.

His assistant? The one he'd started seeing, maybe?

None of the messages particularly caught his eye.

Until he hit the fifth one down, and he read it more carefully.

Trying to seal the deal.

Was "the deal" Cassidy?

Whomever he'd texted—the name only said Fall Guy—responded:

May have to take matters into my own hands.

Ryan responded with:

No, let's stick to the plan.

What was that about? Could Ryan simply have been talking to a coworker? To the task force leader who'd replaced Samuel? Or was there more to these messages?

He had to see if Mac could trace the number.

And he had to do it now.

GREG HAD TIED UP RYAN, and Cassidy's ex-fiancé was now in a matching wooden chair beside her in the living room. Both of them faced Greg like bottles on a makeshift firing range.

The two of them had no time to talk or debrief, not with Greg staring at them. Not with his gun in his hand. Not with the instruments of torture only an arm's reach away.

But Cassidy was keenly aware that Ryan had a blood stain across the front of his shirt, a cut across his eye, and a swollen cheek.

She could only imagine what Greg had done to him.

Cassidy waited, expecting Greg to begin his torture. His interrogation. His process.

Instead, he walked to the door, like he was on a mission.

"I've got one more thing to do before the fun gets started," he announced.

Another shot of fear rushed through Cassidy. What else could Greg possibly have to do? He had the two people he wanted right in front of him. There was no one else who had any value to him.

Except . . . maybe . . . Ty.

She sucked in a quick breath at the thought.

Ty wasn't a part of this, yet Cassidy had *made* him a part of it. He knew information. He could be seen as a threat. Would Greg really pull him into this nightmare?

Cassidy could hardly stomach the thought, but it was the only possibility she could fathom—and it was a horrible possibility.

She jerked against the ropes around her, knowing it was no use but trying anyway. Greg only smiled and stepped toward the door.

"Have fun," he muttered. "But don't wear yourself out. You'll need that energy later."

With one last glance at them, Greg stepped outside and shut the door.

As soon as he was gone, Cassidy turned to Ryan. "Are you okay?"

He nodded, but his expression looked haggard. "I was out looking for you. I pulled into the convenience store—I was going to ask the employees if they'd seen you. Before I could, someone jumped me, and everything went black."

"I'm glad you're okay." The rest of what Ryan had said settled on her. "People are out looking for me?"

"They are. I guess someone sent Ty a text, claiming it

was from you and that you'd left town. He didn't buy it."

A burst of relief filled Cassidy. That was Ty. Thank goodness, he didn't take things at face value.

But now Greg might be out there looking for him.

Cassidy jerked against the ropes again, even though she knew it was futile. If she could just reach one of those scalpels . . . maybe she could undo her ropes. Maybe they could get out of here before Greg returned again.

Cassidy leaned forward, trying to inch out of the coils of rope around her. It did no good.

She tried to rise to her feet, to move forward with the chair attached. But the piece of furniture was too heavy.

She tried walking it back and forth. But the wood was just too thick and awkward.

She needed to do something to gain the upper hand, though.

"What are you doing?" Ryan asked.

"Trying to figure out some way to get out of here."

"It doesn't appear to be working."

He was right. It wasn't.

Cassidy stopped to catch her breath, her thoughts racing ahead—racing to Ryan. "Why does Greg want you here, Ryan? Why not let you go?"

"I suppose it's better if they wipe out the prosecuting attorney and the lone witness." Ryan frowned, as if the thought left a bad taste in his mouth. "He probably thinks I know too much."

Her thoughts continued to race ahead. "But there's something that doesn't make sense. This guy—Greg—he keeps asking me for information. I don't know what he's talking about."

Even though Cassidy had an inkling, she didn't share her theories. Not yet.

"You don't have anything that might be beneficial to the other side? Something that would make them look bad?" Ryan glanced at her, blood trickling down his forehead and into his eyes.

Cassidy cringed at the sight.

She was designed to fight. She'd been trained. Conditioned. Tested.

But Ryan was trained to use his mind in battle. His words. His logic.

It didn't seem fair that he was being brought into this battle also.

Then again, DH-7 had never been accused of playing fair.

She licked her lips, contemplating her next words. At this point, neither of them would probably get out of here—not unless they acted fast.

Ideas rolled around in her mind. She didn't have time to entertain them properly. She was going to have to rely on gut instinct to get through this.

"I have something that Samuel sent me," she finally said. "But if Samuel sent this . . . this . . . evidence to me, then these guys already have the information. They don't need it from me. That's what doesn't make sense."

"What did he send you?" Ryan asked.

She licked her lips again. "Just some information I requested, all bundled nicely on a jump drive. I'm sure there are multiple copies of it floating out there. I can't understand why he'd need the copy I have."

"That's a good question. I don't know the answer. Because you're right—whatever you most likely have, I'm sure there are copies at the PA's office." He paused. "Unless Samuel sent something extra."

A few seconds ticked by in silence. Cassidy's thoughts continued to roll like the tumultuous ocean waves. Even mentioning that jump drive was risky—like going into the water with a deadly undertow dragging her to a near certain death. She knew all too well what that felt like.

"I've heard there's fracturing within DH-7," Ryan finally said.

"Samuel mentioned that."

Ryan cast her a weary glance. "It's probably better if you don't trust most of what Samuel told you."

"How did you discover he double-crossed you?" Cassidy sure hadn't seen any signs.

"We have another inside guy with DH-7," Ryan said. "He hasn't been as successful as you, but he's kept us in the loop about things going on. He came across the information."

Samuel had mentioned that the task force had someone else undercover, but Cassidy had never heard a name. "Who? Who is this man?"

The guy must be good because Cassidy had been in

the trenches, and she'd had no inkling the police had another guy undercover. It would have been nice to know, nice to have someone to fall back on.

"You know I can't tell you," Ryan said.

Cassidy had figured he would say that. The issue seemed so inconsequential right now with both of their lives on the line. "So this informant told you that the leadership of DH-7 is fracturing, and that Samuel has something to do with it?"

"We believe Samuel was on DH-7's side all along—on their payroll. But we also believe he started to have second thoughts. That's probably why he sent you that information." Ryan paused and lowered his voice. "Samuel may be dead now. We're not sure."

"Dead? I thought you said he was missing."

Cassidy felt around behind her, trying to reach something she could use to fray the ropes around her wrists. She glanced over her shoulder. Behind her, there was an old paperweight with a seashell on it. A remote. Some fingernail clippers.

Fingernail clippers? Those might be her best bet.

If only she could reach them.

She strained her muscles, her limbs, desperate to reach something to help her out of this situation. After a moment, her fingers connected with metal.

She'd gotten them!

"There was a warrant out for Samuel," Ryan said, not seeming to notice what she was doing. "If the FBI found him, he probably didn't survive. He'd rather die than be taken into custody."

"Even if that's true, it still doesn't explain why Greg wants this jump drive so badly."

"It probably has names. Maybe he wants to destroy all the copies as a safeguard."

"All the names were all coded." Cassidy began working the sharp tip of the nail cutters against the rope. It would be a slow process, but at least it was something.

"Maybe you should just give the jump drive to him. See if he'll let us go."

She jerked her gaze toward Ryan. "You and I both know that will never happen. We're dead either way. Why give him what he wants first?"

"It might save us some pain." As Ryan said the words, he hung his head, almost like he was physically done—like the toll on him had already been too high.

Cassidy shrugged. "I doubt it."

If Greg's mind was made up to torture them, he was going to torture them.

She worked the clippers harder.

"Could you tell Ty where this information is?" Ryan said. "He could bring it. Maybe we could plan our escape somehow that way. Use it as leverage."

"I don't want to pull Ty into this." Cassidy paused. "Besides, he doesn't know about the jump drive. No one does. And I hid it."

Ryan's eyes brightened, as if he'd found the perfect solution. "You could get a message to Ty. Tell him where you hid it."

"How would I get a message to him?" Maybe that head injury was getting to Ryan.

"I don't know. Maybe we could think of some way."

"It doesn't really matter. Ty could figure it out, even if I didn't tell him." The words tasted bad in her mouth. Cassidy wanted Ty to stay out of this, yet she'd put him in the very position she wanted to avoid.

"What does that mean?"

"It means I put it somewhere something else was hidden in the past. It made the most sense." She resisted spelling it all out for Ryan. The spot was her secret, and it would be nice to keep it that.

"You're losing me."

Cassidy let out a long sigh and considered her response. Maybe Ryan was right. Maybe she *should* tell Greg. He could go retrieve the jump drive, and that would buy her more time to figure out how to escape.

She felt like she was in the middle of one of her father's poker games right now, and that her next move could either destroy her or offer the biggest winnings of her life.

"I found this journal earlier this month in my ice cream truck," Cassidy started. "It made the most sense that I would hide it there, behind the dash." As soon as the words left her lips, she regretted them. "I shouldn't have told you that. Now you're at risk also."

"It's not like I'm going anywhere."

"I don't think either of us are." Cassidy sighed and leaned her head back, a million thoughts clashing inside. She put the information out there. Now she needed to wait. "What happened to Rachel Edwards?"

Rachel had been the prosecuting attorney of King County before Ryan, but she'd been killed by DH-7. The gang's rampage after their leader Raul died had been deadly and hazardous for more than one person. The memory of it all made Cassidy's heart pang with regret.

She scraped the clippers more, feeling the rope beginning to fray.

Ryan frowned. "Rachel officially died in a car crash, but we all know it was no accident. DH-7 was trying to get her out of the way. They made attempts on my life as well, but I had a security team around me until I came here."

Cassidy studied his face, trying to read his thoughts, to figure out what he was thinking about throughout this conversation. They still had so much to talk about. Ryan had answers that she needed.

"I never imagined just how deep I was getting into this when I took that assignment," Cassidy muttered. It's like they said: hindsight is twenty-twenty. She'd been so hungry for success, so hungry to make a difference, that she'd charged forward, not giving enough thought to how this would turn her life upside down.

"I don't think you could have understood it," Ryan said. "The scope of all this is huge, and there's no lengths these guys won't go to in order to get what they want."

"It just boils down to money and power, doesn't it?

Isn't that what's at the core of this group?" It was a deadly motivation.

"I guess you could say that. People would do a lot to obtain those two things. You can do anything you want with money and power."

"But they'll cost you your soul. I've seen that first-hand." Images of her life growing up filled her thoughts. They'd had everything at their fingertips—except happiness. Stuff couldn't buy people content-ment. Power didn't change diagnoses.

It had taken Cassidy's life being turned upside down for her to see it.

"I'm sure you have experienced it indirectly," Ryan said. "Not many people grow up in one of the richest families in the US."

"It wasn't all it's made out to be." She frowned.

"I would have killed for that when I was a kid. We ate beans and cereal every day. It was all we had money for."

Cassidy glanced over at him, seeing a different side of him emerge. "You never told me that before when we were dating."

"I wasn't proud of it."

"There's nothing to be ashamed about. Money doesn't define us."

"You're really not that naïve, are you?"

Cassidy felt her back muscles tightening. "I'm not naïve. I've had a change of perspective."

"Well, in my part of the world, money is everything. I don't ever want to be poor again."

"Maybe you should have gone into private practice then." Her words contained more than a touch of annoyance. She had more important things to think about now. Things like getting out of here.

TY COULDN'T STOP PACING on the grass outside the general store. Anxiety wound tighter and tighter around his spine, like a coiling snake, with every minute that passed.

While Quinton searched Ryan's vehicle for trace evidence, Mac was inside Swanner's looking at security camera footage.

Ty reviewed what he knew so far, starting with the fact that Ryan was now missing or possibly dead. The man had sent some questionable texts, the ones that Ty had found on his phone, and the wording was suspect. Ty supposed those texts could be related to Ryan's job— but maybe not. Samuel might be the bad guy who'd betrayed the FBI.

And, of course, the bigger fact was this: Cassidy might be on this island, but Ty had no idea where.

He wanted to run around, searching for her. But Mac had reminded him that it would do no good. He would only exhaust himself, and the chances he'd find her that way were slim.

Ty needed a more thought-out, concentrated method.

But thinking things out wasn't his forte right now. He'd rather use brute force.

How had these guys found her? What had Cassidy told him Ryan said about how he'd located her?

It had been that video of the guys on flakka, terrorizing people on the boardwalk here in Lantern Beach.

As he waited, he did a search for the images on his phone. They weren't hard to find.

He watched the video play, remembering that day all too well.

Someone had given three men a super-enhanced strain of the drug. They'd looked—and acted—like zombies. One had even tried to bite someone. He and Cassidy had stepped in. They'd had no other choice.

As he watched the video, he paused.

He could clearly see both him and Cassidy rushing in to help. But Cassidy had been wearing a baseball cap and sunglasses. Her hair was now long and blonde and wavy, unlike when she'd been in Seattle. Her hair then was long, dark, and straight and often pulled into a bun. In her old life, she'd been button-up and professional. Here, she wore loose clothing and jean shorts.

In this video, she was moving quickly—too quickly to make out the details of her face.

Still, this was just one video.

There were more as tourists had rushed to capture everything on camera.

Ty clicked through a few other videos but saw more of the same.

It was nearly impossible to make out any details. And nothing about the woman in those video frames resembled the person Cassidy used to be.

Was Ryan just unusually observant?

Or was there more to his story?

Mac rounded the corner from the front of the store and walked toward Ty. "Someone just called the department. She said that Mr. Hinkle's house has had a lot of activity this evening. Said it might not be unusual, except for the fact that Mr. Hinkle hasn't been there in five years."

Ty's blood surged. Maybe this was their first real lead as to where someone had taken Cassidy. "Let's go."

The minutes seemed to be ticking by, moving through gelatin, as Cassidy and Ryan sat in the old cabin, tied to the heavy wooden chairs.

What was Greg doing? Cassidy wondered. When would he be back? And what would he do when he returned?

Ryan had been sitting silently beside her, his head drooping as if he were tired. Cassidy let him have his space. It gave her time to contend with her own thoughts. To continue to dig at the rope around her wrists. To pray and to pray hard.

Finally, after several minutes of quiet, Ryan raised his head. "We were a great team, Cassidy."

Her stomach turned at his words. He must be remembering differently than she was. "Not really."

"What was wrong with us?"

She sagged slightly against the chair, her adrenaline beginning to fade. Her body wanted to crash, and her exhaustion doubled at Ryan's question. "For starters, we had to keep our relationship a secret."

"I explained why." His voice sounded all logical and without emotion. "Your dad is a polarizing figure, and I didn't want that to affect my election."

Cassidy frowned, wondering why they were even talking about this. Yet she couldn't stop herself. "Ideally, you're proud of the person you're dating, even if their family might hurt your election campaign."

"Touché."

"Besides, don't deny that you're interested in your assistant. It's as clear as day in those photos."

Ryan glanced at her. "So you kept tabs on me?"

"Before I called things off." This conversation was getting old, and Cassidy knew she should end it.

"Ouch."

"I mean, you really think I'm going to believe that you lost your cell phone and could think of no other way to be in touch?"

He narrowed his eyes as if annoyed with the fact

that Cassidy doubted him. "I really did lose it. I even wondered if someone stole it."

"And you didn't think to report that? Someone could have traced my number and found me."

"Well, they didn't, did they? The person who wants to kill you is someone who knew your location all along. Besides, I thought maybe it was working out for the best that we weren't in touch. Especially after Rachel died. I figured someone could go after me and, like you said, trace you through that phone."

Cassidy wasn't sure she bought it, but the explanation did have some plausibility. She didn't respond—it wasn't worth the effort.

"We're going to get through this," Ryan said. "We'll get out of here. You can come back to Seattle. Everyone on the force will think you're a super star. They already talk about your new name as Commotio Cordis."

"I don't want to be a super star. And I don't see myself going back to Seattle." Nor did Cassidy see herself getting out of this, but she didn't bother to say that.

"Why's that?"

"Because I love it here." She glanced at Ryan and saw that his wounds had stopped bleeding. Maybe they weren't as deep as Cassidy had feared. That was a small bit of good news.

"How can you love a little island? You won't ever get anywhere here. Not career-wise."

"Maybe the key to happiness isn't always advancing in your career. Have you ever considered there's more to life than that?" She didn't want to sound judgmental or superior—she really didn't. But Ryan's attitude was grating on her.

"Not really."

"And that's one more reason it's a good thing we broke up." How much time had passed? How long had Greg been gone? At least an hour. Maybe more.

"You've changed," Ryan said after a few minutes of silence.

"For the better."

"I'm not so sure about that. You have so much potential, Cassidy. Why waste it? Why throw it all away for some guy?"

She cut him a sharp glance. "I'm not throwing it all away, for one thing. And Ty isn't just some guy."

"I have to admit . . . that kind of hurts. I always wanted to be the one you said stuff like that about."

Cassidy didn't buy it. "You've already found your true love—your job."

"Why do I think that's not a compliment?"

Before she could respond, the door knob jiggled. A moment later, Greg stepped inside. He smiled in a way that had Cassidy instantly feeling suspicious—and on guard.

He held something between his fingers.

Was that a . . . jump drive?

Cassidy felt the blood leave her face.

Ryan struggled against the ropes around him, as if he wanted to jump up and attack Greg. "What did you do?"

"You don't think I was just going to leave the two of you here to chat without using it to my advantage, did you? I left a bug here, so I could listen to every word you said."

Cassidy gritted her teeth before saying, "So you heard where I left the information?"

Greg's smile widened. "That's right. And there's no one at your house because they're all out looking for you. Worked out well."

She sawed the ropes even more vigorously, scraping the clippers against the threads. "They're going to find me. You're not going to get away with this."

She cringed at her words, knowing good and well she sounded like the hapless victim from every melodramatic cop show on TV.

"We'll see about that." With a new gait to his step, Greg went to his laptop computer, opened it, and stuck the thumb drive into the port.

Cassidy held her breath as she waited to see how all of this would play out. She'd suspected this scenario might materialize, and she'd planned accordingly. It was a risky move, and she wasn't sure if it would keep her alive or kill her.

Go big or go home.

Ryan exchanged a glance with her.

At once, she was taken back to her final day at the DH-7 compound. She remembered that picture of the heart that had only hours earlier belonged to a living, breathing person. She remembered feeling a fear so deep she'd nearly drowned in it, unable to claw her way back to the surface.

That same fear invaded her now.

As if her heart understood the danger, it pounded rapidly into her chest—too rapidly. Greg might not have to kill her. Her body might just shut down on its own.

If I die, at least I know I died doing the right thing. The noble thing.

And even if no one knows my sacrifice, it won't matter. This was never about recognition.

Still, Cassidy continued to hold her breath and waited for the details to pop onto the screen. She waited for Greg's reaction. Waited for the fallout.

"What?" Greg pounded his fist against the table. "What is this? Pictures of the beach? Of sunrise and sunset? Of a dog?"

"Did I get my jump drives mixed up?" This was no time to be smart. Yet Cassidy couldn't seem to stop herself. And she didn't have anything better to say at the moment. She wasn't ready yet to confess.

Greg stormed toward her, anger raging in his eyes. He drew his arm back, his hand in a ball, and then lunged his fist into the side of Cassidy's face. "I never knew you were such a smart mouth."

Cassidy's face throbbed, and stars flashed in her eyes. "You didn't think I was going to give it up that easily, did you?"

She'd suspected from the moment Greg left that he may have planted a listening device in this place. It had been a brilliant move on his part. Thankfully, Cassidy was a step ahead of him.

She'd known from the moment she got that jump drive just how valuable it was. Even then, she'd come up with a plan to make sure it never got into the wrong hands.

Greg pulled out his gun and aimed it at her. "Where is it?"

"You're going to have to kill me."

Courage is not lack of fear. It's facing your fears.

Right now, Cassidy was staring her fears right in the eye.

Greg turned until his gun pointed at Ryan. "Then I'll kill him. And after I kill him, I'll kill your boyfriend and anybody else I can find that you remotely care about."

Cassidy's throat went dry. Threaten her? She could handle it. She'd dug her own grave.

But threaten people she cared about? That was an entirely different story.

Greg stepped closer. "You're going to tell me where that jump drive is. And after you give me that information, you're going to call your parents."

"Why would I do that?"

"Because I have a ransom demand. They either send us money, or you die." He smiled. "Unfortunately, you'll die either way."

His words confirmed what Cassidy already suspected. She was chosen for this job for more than one reason. It wasn't necessarily her skill. No, it had also been for her parents' money and influence.

As he stepped away and Cassidy caught his profile, she sucked in a breath.

"You're Tyron," she muttered.

He turned toward her, a satisfied gleam in his eyes. "It took you a while."

"You were the DEA agent who was undercover." Everything clicked in her mind. How had she not seen this earlier?

"That's right. I'm also the one who sold you out to Raul. I let him know that you hadn't really killed Samantha."

"Why would you do that?"

"You were supposed to die that night. Instead, you killed Raul and messed up all our plans."

Just when Cassidy thought all her hope was gone, the door crashed open.

WITH GUNS DRAWN, Ty and Mac threw open the door to the old cottage and invaded the space.

Ty held his breath, fully expecting to find Cassidy.

Instead, three teenagers sat on an old couch with beer bottles in one hand and joints in the other.

They all jumped to their feet, sloshing their drinks onto their laps. Their hands flew in the air, and dazed expressions crossed their faces, barely perceptible in the hazy, dark space.

"What in tarnation are you doing here?" Mac asked, lowering his gun.

One guy—probably in his late teens—with long dark dreadlocks, baggy jean shorts, and a ripped white T stepped forward as the group's leader. "Nothing. We didn't mean nothing, man. We just needed a place for privacy."

"Don't call me man," Mac said. "Show some respect, and call me chief."

"Yes, sir . . . chief." The boy nearly snarled as he said the words.

"So you broke in?" Mac continued.

The boy shrugged, like he didn't have a worry in the world. "No one lives here. Last time we went to the shore, and the beach patrol showed up. This seemed like a better bet."

"Do you own this place?"

"No."

"Then you broke in."

"Look, man—I mean, sir. I'm sorry," he said. "We'll leave. Please just don't tell my parents."

Ty's heart sank. This had seemed like their best lead. But this wasn't connected to Cassidy's case at all.

Which meant they were no closer to finding her.

He knew with every second that passed, Cassidy was closer to death. And that wasn't okay.

Cassidy held her breath as she stared at the splintered door.

Samuel stood in the entry.

Alive.

With a gun in his hand.

Was he here to help . . . or . . .

"Stop what you're doing and put your hands up," Samuel growled, looking more rugged than Cassidy had ever seen him with unshaven cheeks and sloppy clothes. "Right now."

Greg froze, but slowly turned his gun until it faced Samuel.

Who was on whose side?

She wasn't sure. For a moment, she felt like she was back in the ocean the evening she was snatched. Back to feeling as if she was trying to swim one way while the current pulled her another.

She needed to listen very carefully and watch as things played out over the next few minutes.

"Samuel Stephens." Ryan's voice cracked with tension. "How'd you find us?"

"It wasn't easy." Samuel gave him a pointed look. "Thanks to you."

"Don't listen to him, Cassidy," Ryan snapped. "He's working for DH-7. Don't forget."

Samuel still held the gun steady, aimed at Greg, daring him to make one wrong move. "That's not true, Cassidy. You're a smart girl. You can put the pieces together."

That was exactly what she was trying to do. But Cassidy didn't feel especially insightful at the moment. No, her thoughts collided inside her.

Loyalty against knowledge.

Desire against reality.

Hope against the sobering truth.

She watched Greg, trying to gauge if he had allegiance to Samuel. Or had Samuel really betrayed him as well?

Nothing was clear.

"Greg and Ryan are both here to try to get the information I sent you." Samuel's voice sounded deep and left no room for questions. He was the consummate FBI agent—someone who'd given his life for the job. Someone others had looked up to. Someone who always got the job done.

Could Cassidy trust him now? Were Greg and Ryan really working together?

"Don't listen to him," Ryan said. "He's trying to turn you against me. Look at me. Would I have gotten myself beat-up like this? You know that's ludicrous."

"When the stakes are this high, nothing is ludicrous," Samuel said.

Cassidy's head pounded harder. Any way she looked at it, either man could be guilty.

And why was Greg being so quiet? Did he not want to let on that he was working for either man?

"I don't know what's going on," Cassidy started. "But somewhere on this path, things went terribly wrong. I thought we were all working for the good of the people we serve. I can see that's not the case."

"The very man who's overseeing the trial over this case is actually the one who's calling all the shots for the defense," Samuel said. "I just discovered Ryan's involvement last week. I started digging a little deeper after my last conversation with you, Cassidy. Ryan here didn't like that and tried to have me killed."

"Don't listen to him, Cassidy." Ryan struggled against his binds. "He's just trying to turn you against me. He's trying to get the evidence you found thrown out."

But what Samuel said made more sense. His time-line made sense.

Would Ryan really sink this low? Could he possibly be involved with DH-7? He was in charge of overseeing the justice system for citizens in and around Seattle. Would he really compromise himself like this?

"Remember Tango Mango, Cassidy." Samuel's gaze flickered to Cassidy, but only for a second. "That was what your friend Lucy's dad used to call her, right?"

"Right." Where was he going with this? Why was he bringing up Lucy?

"Ryan's uncle is the brains behind DH-7," Samuel continued. "He passed the torch down to Ryan. Ryan's family is responsible for the murder of your friend."

A small cry escaped her lips. "No . . ."

Could someone she'd once cared about—Ryan—be responsible for the most devastating loss in her life?

"He's playing with your head, Cassidy." Ryan struggled against his ropes again, grunting and twisted to no avail. "You know my family. You know they'd never be involved with something like that."

"I know your parents. They're the only ones I've ever met. But didn't your dad say something one time about your mom's brother being the black sheep of the family? I never asked you about that. I figured it wasn't my business."

"He was the black sheep because he decided to pursue a degree in art. He lives in a little apartment with four other creatives. You know my parents. They don't take things like that seriously. Uncle Rob *was* a black sheep."

Who should Cassidy trust? Both of the men made sense. Yet her gut reminded her of what she knew all along.

Movement caught her attention at the corner of her eye.

She turned in time to see Greg aim his gun.

And then she heard a shot fill the air.

TY AND MAC were still standing outside the small cottage the three potheads had invaded when they heard gunfire in the not-so-far distance.

One glance between Mac and Ty was all it took to show their agreement.

"Let's go," Mac said. "I'll deal with these delinquents at another time."

They jumped into Mac's car and took off toward the noise.

"It sounded close." Blood pounded in Ty's ears. "Maybe a couple of streets over."

"This is the area where there are a lot of old houses dating back to the fifties. People who own them might only come a few times a year. We just need to look for one that's occupied and shouldn't be."

They sped that direction. Ty felt ready to crawl out of his skin. He thought he was done facing war when he left the military. Little did he know he'd be facing his biggest battles here on US soil.

The first street yielded nothing—no strange cars, lights, or evidence of the gunfire. Nor did the second.

But on the third street, Mac cut his headlights and rolled to a stop as he neared a house at the end of the lane.

"Will Preston owns that place." He pointed to a house in the distance. "He only comes for one week a year. And notice there are two cars out front? Well, Will is from Pennsylvania. Neither of those cars have PA plates."

"Let's go then."

Mac opened his door. "Follow my lead. I know Cassidy's your lady, but we need to be rational here."

"Of course." Ty prayed he'd be able to restrain himself because all he wanted to do right now was rush inside that house and see if Cassidy was there. To make sure that gunfire hadn't been directed at her. Or . . .

He cringed.

He couldn't finish the thought. Of course the bullet hadn't hit her.

Please, God. No . . .

But the situation was precarious, at best, and Ty would be a fool not to acknowledge that the outcome of this might not be what he wanted.

He'd known from the moment Cassidy told him her secret that things would get harder before they got easier.

Maybe he hadn't quite grasped just how much harder, though.

He drew the gun he'd brought—Cassidy's gun—and tried to prepare himself for what he might find inside.

Each possibility seemed like too much to stomach, though.

Suddenly, he heard something crash. Then crash again.

And then he heard Cassidy shout, "No!"

Mac pushed through the door, his gun drawn. Ty was right behind him.

They both froze at what they saw inside.

Total chaos.

Blood.

And a game of quick draw.

Cassidy flipped the chair behind her and smashed it to the floor. As soon as she did, the ropes around her loosened. Her adrenaline had kicked back in and given her a temporary burst of strength.

Ryan had somehow managed to get his ropes off, as well. How had he done that so quickly? It didn't matter right now.

They all stood there staring at each other, facing off.

Except for Greg.

When he'd pivoted, Samuel had shot him. Blood

gushed from his shoulder as he lay on the floor. He'd groaned with pain for a moment before going still.

He wasn't dead, but he appeared to be unconscious. He'd need medical help. And soon. He was losing too much blood.

"Everyone needs to calm down," Cassidy muttered.

As soon as she said the words, the door flew open.

Mac and Ty flooded inside.

Her heart turned to honey.

Ty.

He was okay.

And he was here.

Which meant he could be in the line of fire.

The honey instantly hardened.

Ryan grabbed Greg's gun, pointing it at Samuel, who still held his own gun.

Meanwhile, Mac's gun was on Samuel and Ty's on Ryan.

Cassidy remained empty-handed.

"Are you okay, Cassidy?" Ty asked.

She nodded, not daring to move. Not with this much tension in the air. One wrong move, and they could all die.

"Cassidy, you've got to believe me." Ryan moved away from her and took a more secure stance apart from the rest of them. "I'm on your side. Samuel just pulled the trigger on Greg to eliminate him. He knew Greg could implicate him in this investigation."

"Cassidy, I think you know the truth," Samuel said. "There's a reason Ryan didn't call you back. Because he was working for DH-7. Not to mention dating his assistant."

"Don't listen to him," Ryan said. "He wants to turn you against me."

"Now look here." Mac's voice cut through the room, tinged with aggravation. "'I'm the chief around these parts, and I demand that you all put down your weapons. Now."

No one moved.

"I figured that was too easy," Mac muttered, scowling at everyone in the room. "We're going to have to do things the hard way, aren't we?"

"What's going on, Cassidy?" Ty asked. "Talk to us."

Where did she even start? She glanced around at each of the players here. "One of these guys is working for DH-7. More like, DH-7 is working for him. Samuel and Ryan both have motives and evidence to tie them to the group."

"Who do you think is behind it?" Mac asked.

Cassidy's thoughts raced through her mind as her gaze bounced back and forth from Ryan to Samuel. They both had motive, means, and opportunity. One wrong call on her part, and this could all end very, very badly.

"It's hard to say," she muttered.

"Trust your gut, Cassidy." Ty's voice sounded calm and reassuring. "You have good instincts. You always have."

She loved how much he believed in her.

"Enough of this talk," Ryan snapped. "I need to get

Cassidy out of here. She's not safe. That's what I was trying to tell you all along. Samuel probably has backup on the way here now, and then we'll all be sitting ducks."

"Ryan is going to kill you once he gets you away from here," Samuel said. "Greg is working for him. This was all an act, Cassidy."

Her head pounded.

No, she was overthinking this. Cassidy knew who was guilty. In her gut she did—just like Ty had told her.

But how could she throw out the accusation without someone getting hurt?

In a split second, Ryan's gun turned toward Ty.

"No!" Cassidy grabbed the first thing she could find.

The seashell paperweight.

She jerked her arm back and threw it across the room.

The rock hit Ryan's hand, and he dropped the gun.

Mac fired at him, but Ryan ducked.

Cassidy dove for the gun on the floor. Her fingers wrapped around the barrel. Before she could grab it, Ryan swooped down also.

She was too late.

In one move, Ryan grabbed the gun and Cassidy's arm. The next thing she knew, the barrel was to her head, and Ryan faced everyone else. Danger pulsated in the room.

"One move, and I'll shoot her. You know I mean it." Even Ryan's voice sounded different as he said the words. Less cultured, more street smart.

"Don't do anything rash," Ty said. "Let her go, and let's talk this through."

"There's nothing to talk through. This is it. The end. Put your guns down."

No one moved.

"I said put your guns down!" Ryan fired at the ceiling, his nostrils flaring.

The sound of the gun rang in Cassidy's ears until she could hardly hear anything else.

Samuel, Mac, and Ty lowered their weapons.

"Now tie them up, Cassidy," Ryan ordered. "And don't try anything funny. Start with your boyfriend."

Her hands were shaking as she grabbed the very ropes that had bound her earlier. She mouthed "I'm sorry" to Ty as she wrapped the ropes around him.

"I love you, Cassidy," he whispered.

"I love you too." She tied the rope as hard as she could, knowing Ryan would check it. But she'd also pressed her fingers into Ty's spine, indicating he should arch his back. That way, when no one was looking, he could slip the ropes off more easily.

"Move faster!" Ryan ordered.

"I'm trying to do it right," Cassidy muttered. "I thought you'd be happy about that."

"I won't be happy until you're dead and buried. And taking the blame for all of this."

Cassidy's steps slowed. "You think people are going to buy the idea that I was behind all of this?"

Thunder cracked outside. The storm was getting closer.

"You even have the tattoo to prove it." Ryan smiled.

"You told them to do this?" She touched the lightning bolt behind her ear. Members of DH-7 had drugged her, and when she'd awoken this tattoo had been there.

"Keep walking!" Ryan growled. "And, yes, of course I did. All of this was planned—including your involvement. We picked you as a pawn."

Under the gun, she tied up Samuel and Mac, mouthing sorry to them as well.

As soon as she was done, Ryan grabbed her arm and dragged her out the door.

"RYAN, WHY WOULD YOU DO THIS?" Cassidy asked, desperate to get through to him as he dragged her through the woods.

Water waited on the other side of the tree line. She could hear it. Smell it. Almost taste it.

It was like the seawater was becoming part of her blood.

What would Ryan do with her once they hit the water? She'd essentially be trapped with nowhere to go unless she wanted to face stormy waters again.

Did she really want to know what Ryan had planned?

"Why would I do this?" Ryan barked. "It's called a legacy. It's called justice."

"You're going to leave a legacy as prosecuting attorney. Why this?" More branches hit her in the face. The forest was thick. Damp. And very much alive.

"There's no money in that job," he said, not slowing

down. "Overseeing the operations of DH-7? I have more money than I could ever dream about."

"And that's it? Seems like a pretty shallow motive."

He scowled. "My uncle was sent to prison, and he was killed there by a member of an opposing gang. People shouldn't go to prison for drugs. They should have the freedom to do what they want to their own bodies. They aren't hurting anyone else."

The air felt sweltering around them, and sweat covered Cassidy's skin. In the distance, she could see glowing eyes.

Frogs.

They silenced their songs as Ryan and Cassidy got closer.

"You know drugs are the gateway to other crimes," Cassidy continued, her lungs still rattling from her near-death experience in the ocean earlier. "People lose their inhibitions. Half the people police pick up are high or drunk. That's why most drugs are illegal because people are a danger to others while under the influence."

"You grew up with everything. You have no room to talk about any of this."

"Is that why I was chosen for this assignment?" she asked. "Is it because of my parents?"

"You have no idea, do you?"

"No idea about what?"

He scoffed. "It was your dad who put my uncle away for life—and that fact ultimately cost my uncle his life since he was killed by a rival gang in prison."

"My dad? What did he have to do with any of this?"

"Your dad provided funding for some special forensic tests that proved my uncle was involved in three shootings."

"He did?" Why hadn't she ever heard about this?

"He did. I guess when your friend Lucy died, your dad wanted to do something to bring her justice. He began giving a good portion of money to the police—money that helped fund things they otherwise couldn't afford."

A surge of pride welled in her. "I see."

"I'm still planning on milking the fact that your parents are filthy rich as much as I can. I should be able to get several million out of your folks. I'll feed that money back into the organization, so we can produce more drugs and make more money. It will be the ultimate irony—and true justice."

"You're deplorable."

"I've been called worse."

"How is taking me going to help you?"

"You're my leverage."

The trees cleared and, just as Cassidy suspected, dark water lurked on the other side. Around the water were marsh grasses on one side and old, weather-worn stumps on the other.

And a boat floated just beyond that. A motorboat. One that would be perfect for escape. Except for the incoming storm.

"What are you doing with me?" Cassidy's voice cracked.

For the first time, Cassidy realized that Ryan just might get away with this. He might put her on that boat and get out of town before anyone could stop him.

If the storm didn't take them.

She could feel the incoming front in the air. The leaves clattered. The seagrass whispered. The waves roared their warning across the seascape. The tip of the island was narrow here, and the water on either side connected during storms, leaving a marshy, swamp-like environment.

Cassidy could not get on that boat with Ryan.

Using her last ounce of strength, she turned around and jammed her elbow into Ryan's throat. The distraction was just enough to make him lose focus. The two wrestled with his gun.

Footsteps sounded behind them.

Ryan heard them.

Shoved her.

Cassidy lost her balance and stumbled toward the ground. Her rib cage hit one of the old stumps sticking out from murky water.

Pain throbbed through her. The breath left her lungs, and stars spun in her head.

"Ryan . . ." she muttered.

She glanced over and saw him running for his boat. There was too much distance between him and Samuel and Ty. He might actually get away.

She heard water sloshing. A motor starting.

She tried to sit up. To chase him. But her rib cage pulsated with pain.

Samuel appeared in her vision, going after Ryan. He'd be too late.

Another set of footsteps stopped near her.

Ty appeared. "Cassidy . . ."

Lightning struck in the distance, and a brisk wind swept over the landscape. The first smattering of rain felt like bullets on her skin.

"I need to get you out of here," Ty muttered.

She didn't have the strength to argue.

She was safe now, she realized.

For the moment, at least.

And she'd take whatever moments she could get.

Ty stared down at Cassidy, his heart beating out of control as he saw the agony on her face. "Are you okay?"

She nodded, but her eyes weren't focused. Pain invaded their depths, and a haze consumed her features. "I'm fine. Don't worry about me. Did Ryan get away?"

Ty glanced behind him and saw Samuel stop at the waterline. He heard the motor of a boat speeding away, just as lightning lit the sky above them. "It looks like it."

"He had a backup plan," Cassidy muttered.

"You're probably not surprised, are you?"

"No. Not at all. Where's Mac?"

"Keeping an eye on Greg," Ty said. "We didn't want him to get away, in case he regains consciousness."

"Smart thinking."

Ty studied her face, frowning. "I'm going to have to pick you up, Cassidy. It's going to hurt."

"I'll be okay."

Bracing himself, he scooped his arms under Cassidy and slowly stood. Cassidy's face scrunched with pain. She probably had a bruised rib. Maybe a cracked one. He wasn't sure.

From the looks of it, she could hardly catch her breath.

"You're going to be okay," Ty promised her.

"Thanks for finding me, Ty." Her voice sounded stretched thin as she rested her head against his chest."

"I was going to find you or die trying."

Samuel joined them as Ty carried Cassidy through the forest. Leaves still slapped them—the landscape was too thick to avoid it. Bugs still swarmed around them. Rain still fell.

But it didn't matter anymore. All that mattered was that Ty and Cassidy were together.

"I'm sorry I doubted you, Samuel," Cassidy muttered.

"I'm sure Ryan was convincing," Samuel said. "I'm just sorry it all played out like this."

They reached the cabin, and Samuel opened the door. As soon as they stepped inside, Ty knew something was wrong.

Mac stood in the room, scowling and rubbing the back of his head.

"What happened?" Samuel asked.

"I looked away from Greg—but only for a second," Mac explained. "He must have grabbed the scalpel from that tray and shoved it into his own neck."

"Is he . . ." Cassidy's voice cracked.

"He's dead." Mac frowned again.

Greg had been their only way of getting information. Of course, the man would rather die than live with the consequences of his choices.

Samuel shook his head, a mixture of sadness and dull realization spreading over his features. "Greg, Greg, Greg. What did you get yourself into?"

That was the question of the hour.

Ty gently lowered Cassidy onto the couch. Her face twisted with discomfort. But she was alive, and, with some TLC, she should be okay.

Samuel let out a long breath and turned toward her. "We have a lot to talk about, Cassidy."

"I know we do."

Ty nodded. "First, we need to get our story together. We've got to keep parts of this quiet if we want to protect Cassidy's identity—which we do. Authorities will ask a lot of questions."

"Then let's talk," Mac said. "Because the FBI is on their way. We've got a dead body, an abduction, and a killer on the loose. We've got a lot of explaining to do."

FIVE HOURS later—five long hours—Samuel and Cassidy slipped away from the swarms of law enforcement officials to talk. It was still raining outside. Thundering. Lightning. Blowing. But the sun was coming up, and the promise of a new day—albeit a gray, soggy one—lingered on the horizon.

Her ribs still hurt—like crazy. Doc Clemson had come, and, when Cassidy had refused to go to the clinic, he'd preliminarily diagnosed her with a bruised rib. He'd bandaged her midsection and told her to take pain meds for the next few days. He'd also checked her lungs, since she was still coughing after inhaling the water in the ocean, and gave her a list of symptoms to watch out for—symptoms that should send her straight to the hospital.

Ty waited inside with Mac while the FBI questioned them. They'd taken jurisdiction over the scene—and it was just as well. Samuel could control more of the narrative this way.

The scent of fresh rain rose around them. The mugginess of the air mingled with the cool breeze of the storm.

If circumstances were different, Cassidy might enjoy this moment. But, while she rejoiced that Samuel was actually who he claimed to be, the fact remained that Ryan was still out there.

Cassidy's adrenaline had long since worn off, and all she wanted to do was take a long shower and climb into bed.

But as she realized she was about to learn the truth, her blood pumped harder.

Wasn't this what she wanted? What she needed to know?

On the other hand, certainly there would be talk about what came next. Would Samuel tell her to leave Lantern Beach? To start over with a new identity? Cassidy wasn't ready to face that possibility.

"What happened, Samuel?" Cassidy started, unable to wait any longer.

He ran a hand over his aging face. He was in his early fifties, but life had worn him down. Given him more wrinkles than necessary. More gray hairs. More world weariness.

At least he still had a thick head of salt-and-pepper hair, a fit build, and a sharp mind.

"Last time we talked, you mentioned that there was probably a puppet master, correct?" he started.

"Right."

"I started looking into it. About that time, someone approached me. That PI that your parents hired. Ricky Ernest."

"Okay."

"He'd traced you back to DH-7 and figured out you went undercover. He also said he talked to Ryan, and Ryan had hinted he was worried about you and desperate to find you. That didn't ring true to me because Ryan knew exactly what happened."

"Right."

"I began to trace Ryan's history—specifically his uncle. He was heavy into the drug and gang scene. The further I kept on going back, the more connections I began to see with DH-7. So I went to talk to Ryan."

"That couldn't have gone well."

"It didn't. But before I talked to him, I talked to another county attorney about the case. He said the information obtained by you while undercover was unreliable. Apparently, that's what Ryan had told him. But it was the first I'd heard about."

"Ryan was going to sink this case, wasn't he?" Cassidy pulled the blanket around her closer, not necessarily cold but chilled nonetheless. Another agent pulled up and handed them both cups of coffee. Greedily, Cassidy drank hers, desperate for a boost.

"You know it. The only other copy of the evidence was the one I had—and the one I sent to you." Samuel shook his head, his eyes distant as if remembering that day. "Anyway, I went to have a talk with him. He tried to kill me, but I got away. That's when he made up the story about me being an insider for DH-7."

"What about Greg?"

"Greg was working undercover for the DEA. But I knew he was the only one who could have told Ryan some of the details I knew. I had no idea he was secretly working off the books for Ryan."

Cassidy stared into the distance, trying to let everything sink in. It was going to take a while.

"Ryan's not going to disappear and let this go," Cassidy muttered.

Samuel narrowed his eyes. "What do you mean? There's nowhere for him to go. I'll send out a bulletin to the FBI, and there will be a manhunt for him."

"He has resources, Samuel. And he has to kill me in order to move forward. He's not finished. And, by that account, everyone I care about is going to be a target."

Thunder rumbled in the distance. "What do you suggest we do?"

Cassidy looked into the distance. Felt the wind against her face. Tried to breathe deeply—but her lungs hurt too badly.

Greatness is measured by the opposition you've overcome.

Lucy's Day-at-a-Glance.

Cassidy had overcome a lot. But she wasn't done yet. Perhaps her greatest opposition was yet to come.

"I have an idea I want to run past you," Cassidy started. "It's risky, but I think it just might work and end this once and for all."

For the next thirty minutes, Cassidy and Samuel talked on the rickety porch as the storm raged around them. They'd hashed out the details of what they needed to do next.

With the plan in place, Cassidy now had to break the news to Ty. She knew he wouldn't take the update well. But she had to let him know anyway.

By the time the FBI had finally released Ty from questioning, the sun had come out but was well hidden behind the storm clouds still around them. There in the same spot where she and Samuel had talked, Cassidy turned to Ty. She nursed a new cup of coffee. Her hair, tangled from seawater, was plastered to her neck and face.

Every time she took a breath, she inhaled the scent of swamp water. The puddles she'd fallen into smelled so strong and pungent she feared flies would start swarming around her.

She still wanted that shower. Maybe even a nap and a warm breakfast and a good dose of quiet time with Jesus.

Mostly, she wanted to stay with Ty forever.

He reached for her but stopped. As much as she'd like to rest in his arms, she couldn't.

Her ribs hurt way too much.

The good news was that Ty didn't seem to care how she looked.

Or smelled.

Ty squeezed her arm instead. "I'm so glad you're okay, Cassidy. But what's going on? You look like you have something to say."

Dread grew in Cassidy's gut with each minute. "I wish I could say this was over, but it's not."

"What's your next plan of action?"

She pleaded with him with her gaze. "I can't tell you the details. But I need you to trust me."

"What does that mean?"

"It means that Samuel and I figured out a way to end this once and for all."

He stared at her. Blinked. Waited. "What can I do?"

And this was the hard part. "I have to do this alone."

He took a step back, and his jaw hardened. "That's the worst idea ever. You know he'll kill you."

"I don't have a choice. This is between Ryan and me. I know you don't want to hear that, but it's true."

"I'm just supposed to stay here and let you get yourself killed?"

Her heart squeezed. "Not exactly. That's why I said you need to trust me."

He tilted his head and let out a breath. "Cassidy . . ."

"Please."

"Can you at least tell me where you're going?"

She licked her lips. "Atlanta."

Finally, Ty nodded. "Okay."

"I'd lean up to give you a kiss, but my ribs can't handle it."

Ty leaned toward her and brushed his lips against hers. "We'll have time for that later."

"Yes, we will."

She turned as she heard a vehicle headed down the lane. An FBI agent stopped the car before it got too close. A moment later, her friends stepped out.

Ty took her hand, and they walked through the drizzling rain toward the group. They each started to hug her until she pointed to her ribs. Instead, they squeezed her shoulder and rubbed her arm and offered compassionate smiles.

"This wasn't the engagement party I envisioned," Lisa said.

Cassidy offered a weak smile. "Me neither."

"We're glad you're okay," Austin said. "We weren't going to stop looking until we found you."

"I appreciate that," Cassidy said. "More than you could possibly know."

Part of her felt like she was saying goodbye right now. But if her plan worked, maybe that wouldn't be the case.

Cassidy only hoped things didn't go terribly, terribly wrong.

TWENTY-TWO

CASSIDY AND SAMUEL rode down the street in silence. They'd just gotten off the second ferry and were headed away from the Outer Banks and toward Raleigh. From there, they'd hop on the interstate and go to Atlanta. The drive would take twelve hours.

She'd needed a big city when she developed her plan, and she'd wanted it to be as far away from Lantern Beach as possible—yet still within driving distance.

In one way, Cassidy felt like she was leaving part of herself behind. I'll be back, she told herself. Yet, if her plan didn't work, that might not be the case at all.

The good news was that her pain medicine had kicked in. She'd changed into some sweats and a T-shirt from the back of one of the FBI agent's cars. And they'd been able to grab some biscuits from a fast-food joint.

"You've done good, Cassidy." Samuel's deep voice brought a certain kind of comfort and calm to her heart.

"It doesn't feel that great right now." She turned toward him. "This level of corruption within the government? It's disturbing, to say the least."

Samuel took a long sip of his coffee, his eyes on the road. He set his cup back into the holder, his expression pensive. "I know. The sooner Ryan and his guys are behind bars, the better."

"I think Ryan's uncle killed my friend Lucy."

"I think you're correct. When I was looking through the case files, I found a grainy surveillance photo that had been taken several years ago. They looked like two men who were at the ATM at the same time, like strangers, so no one ever put it together."

"But you did?"

"That's right. I did. I went to ask Ryan about it, and he acted skittish."

"You must have really gotten suspicious then." She glanced out the window, as the wipers moved in hyper drive, trying to keep the water off the windshield. Globs of rain sloshed back and forth, almost taunting anyone in their path.

"You bet I did. But I made a fatal mistake. I confronted Ryan."

Cassidy tried to picture how that might have played out. "What did he do?"

"At first, he denied my claim. But then he realized it was doing no good. He pulled out a gun and told me that we were going to walk outside together, calm, cool, and casual. That we were going to get into his car, and I was going to go with him."

"That's never good."

"No, it's not." Samuel took another long sip of coffee. "But when we got out of the building, he ran into a coworker who was quite talkative. I saw my opportunity and ran."

"He said you went into hiding because you were the mole." Cassidy could hear Ryan telling her that. She remembered how easily the lies had slipped from his tongue. It was enough to make her nauseated.

"I figured he'd turn it around on me. And I figured he would come here to Lantern Beach also."

"He said he discovered my location because of that PI my parents hired."

"That could be true. Your parents said they told the guy to back off, but I've talked to Ricky Ernest before. He doesn't like to back off."

Cassidy leaned back against the seat, her eyelids feeling heavy. But she couldn't rest until she had some answers. "How long were you on Lantern Beach?"

"I just got there earlier today. I knew if I tried to buy a plane ticket or do anything else on the grid that Ryan would have his men after me. I suspected Greg was helping Ryan, so I put a trace on his phone, which led me here. That's how I found you tonight."

"I'm glad you did." He'd gotten there at just the right time. A little later, and someone else besides Greg might be dead right now.

"I am too. I'm just sorry I didn't get to you sooner."

"I suspected that Ryan was behind it," Cassidy said. "Then when he kept telling me that maybe I should give up the location of the jump drive, I knew something was up. I figured Greg might be listening, and I knew I needed to buy more time, so I led him to a fake device."

"You actually hid the other jump drive?" Samuel stole a glance at her.

Cassidy nodded. "I sure did. One can never be too careful."

"Brilliant move on your part. I guess Ryan wants all the copies so he can destroy them. Without that evidence, he'll be free and clear. As you probably know, Ryan took over for his uncle. Ryan himself grew up dirt poor, and he clawed his way to the top."

"I just don't understand it, though." Cassidy stared out the window, her thoughts heavy. "He has a respectable job."

"For some people, that's not enough. Sometimes money is never enough. They want more. Their appetite for it is insatiable."

"I guess so."

He glanced at her. "You sure you want to go with this plan?"

"Absolutely. It's the only way I can think of."

"You should get some rest, Cassidy," Samuel said. "We have a long drive, and you're going to need all your energy."

Ty sat at his house and absently rubbed Kujo's head. Austin had offered to come over, but he wanted to be by himself. He needed some time alone to process everything.

He couldn't believe Cassidy was gone. Life felt so empty without her here.

She'll be back.

Ty kept telling himself that. Yet doubt crept in.

He wanted to be with Cassidy. He wanted to help her, not sit on the sidelines. Yet he understood that she needed to do this alone, and Ty wanted to respect her wishes.

"This stinks," he muttered to Kujo.

Kujo nuzzled him, as if he understood Ty's agony.

He stared out his screened-in porch and watched the waves crashing in the distance. Usually, the sight calmed him. But now it only reminded him that Cassidy wasn't here with him.

"I've got it bad," he said to Kujo. "I know I do."

He glanced at his cell phone. He'd pulled it from his pocket earlier and set it on the arm of the wooden porch swing. He had little hope that Cassidy would call.

But another idea churned in his mind.

No, leave it alone, Ty. Let it go. Don't get involved.

Yet he found himself picking up the phone.

While he'd been in Ryan's car—when he'd found the man's cell phone—Ty had jotted down the phone numbers from Ryan's call log. He'd done it just in case.

And now that "just in case" was going to find fruition.

Shoving aside his reservations, he dialed one of the numbers. He knew it was a long shot that this call would prove anything, but he was still going to try.

A moment later, someone answered. "Hello?"

Ty didn't recognize the voice, but he played it off like he did. "It's me."

"Who?"

At least the man was smart enough to ask that.

The breeze blew into the receiver, muffling Ty's voice—which worked in his favor right now. "Do I really need to spell it out for you?"

"No, of course not."

"Good because I don't have much time," Ty said. "And the line is breaking up."

"Is the plan still the same?"

"Part of it."

"Let me guess: the part where we find her and kill her?"

"That's right."

"I listened to the bug you left in the cabin. She's headed to Atlanta. I heard her telling her boyfriend."

What? They knew? Ty's heart plummeted. "Guess where we're going then?"

"You sure you want to kill her?"

The hollow feeling in Ty's gut grew. "Yeah, I'm sure."

"Okay, then. I'll meet you there. And we'll find her."

"That's what I wanted to hear. I'll see you there."

Ty hung up. But knew his promise to Cassidy would be nearly impossible to keep.

TWENTY-THREE
23 WEEKS EARLIER

CADY THOUGHT she might pass out. She stood on the edge of the room—it might as well be the edge of a cliff. Other members stood around also, muttering under their breaths, and sweating profusely. She could smell the pungent odor more than she could see it. A guard was situated at the door, which meant no one was leaving without permission.

Her turn in the examination room was coming.

Her turn to be interrogated here in the filthy underbelly of the converted apartment complex.

Only Raul and Orion were doing the questioning—which seemed like a sure sign they thought Cady was guilty. Usually, she was a part of Raul's trusted inner circle. She should be helping them with this matter, but somehow she'd ended up on the other side of things. Had something happened to tip them off?

And that heart Raul had shown everyone a picture of . . . who did it belong to?

Nausea gurgled in her gut.

Another gang member emerged from the interrogation room with tears streaming down her face.

But at least she was alive.

Still, what had they put her through in there?

Raul's eyes scanned the room until they met Cady's. "You're up."

A quiver of dread quaked inside her.

This was it.

The make-or-break moment.

The instant when everything could change.

Her life could be over, and Cady would have nothing to show for it.

Her feet moved toward the door, toward the room, but her mind felt like it had entered another dimension. Like it wanted to separate from the trauma while it could.

A lone chair sat in the dark room, and the lights were dim. Flickering. Buzzing. The place smelled foul, like something had rotted—kind of like the souls of most of the people involved with DH-7. And there was a brown stain on the floor. Was that dried blood?

Her stomach squeezed harder.

Don't show your nerves, Cady. Don't do it.

Raul placed a heavy hand on her shoulder and pushed her into the chair. Her body felt as stiff as the wooden spindles behind her. She glanced over and saw Orion hunkering in the corner, his eyes glistening like a wolf hiding in the darkness, ready to attack.

"You've been pretty faithful." Raul paced in front of

Cady, his gun tucked into his waistband and a knife on his belt. Red stained his hands.

Cady swallowed harder. Just what had happened in here?

"You even killed Reginald," he continued.

Her throat tightened. Had they somehow discovered she hadn't killed him? That she'd faked his death?

Just like she'd faked Samantha's death.

Raul paused in front of her and sneered. "Would you ever betray us?"

"Why would I do that? DH-7 is my family. Besides, Orion saw me shoot Reginald." She'd actually used a rubber bullet.

"Yet you still work at the drugstore," Raul said.

"I get you drugs."

"You know that's small scale compared to what we do."

"Every bit helps, right?"

"I need you to do us a favor," Raul said.

"Anything." Yet Cady's voice sounded strained. She'd already done too much. She wanted out. Now.

"I need you to figure out the narc."

Her pulse jumped. "How am I supposed to do that?"

"I want you to watch people. You're a woman. People will open up to you more easily."

"Ain't no one going to open up about that." She kept her voice even, using her street dialect she'd perfected. "But maybe I can think of other ways to get it out of them."

Raul leaned close—so close Cady could see the flecks in his beady eyes. That she could smell the nicotine on his breath. Could feel him breathing.

"You know what I like?" he finally hissed. "I like can-do attitudes. I like how you're willing to do whatever it takes."

"Of course." Had this been Cady's test? And was that a fatal mistake?

"You're to report back to me." He straightened and pulled out his knife. He began studying the blade, watching the gleam of its sharp edges in a slur of light from overhead.

She shivered. "Okay."

"If you can't find the narc, I'll have to think it's you."

Panic swirled inside her again. "Why would you assume it's me?"

"Because you have more of an outside connection than most of the people here. You know I take care of my people. Yet you want to take care of yourself."

"I've always taken care of myself."

"Not anymore."

She swallowed hard. "Of course not."

"Good. We're on the same page then. I'm going out of town tonight, but I'll follow up with that when I get back."

"You're leaving now? It's midnight." Why had Cady said that? Bedtime had never stopped Raul before. In fact, he preferred to operate in the darkness.

"It's important," he said. "There's something I want to see with my own eyes."

Cady didn't like the sound of that. "I see."

"Some of my guys are going to go firm up a deal for me across town. Do you want to go?"

"I can." Going was the last thing she wanted to do.

"Actually, you should stay here. Get some rest. Talk to anyone who's still here. Understand? See what you can find out?"

"Got it."

Tonight, as soon as Raul and his guys were gone, Cady was leaving. She was going to get a message to Samuel, and that was it.

She couldn't do this anymore.

She had the information she needed. Her job was done.

And she was ready to take charge of her life. Not as the person she used to be. No, this assignment had changed her. She would be making some improvements.

Her life couldn't be all about her career or making her parents proud or living up to the expectations of others.

No, she needed to find community—a positive community. Not like this gang. She needed to find people who surrounded her with love.

She wasn't sure how she was going to do that. She only knew her first step was getting out of here.

TODAY'S GOALS: END THIS ONCE
AND FOR ALL. TAKE BACK MY
LIFE.

TY HADN'T BEEN able to sleep all night as he'd wrestled with what to do.

Keep his promise to Cassidy? Or save her life?

There weren't many in-betweens.

He'd prayed about it. Argued with himself. Tried to convince himself that he could make the right choice.

Yet he still wasn't sure.

As soon as he'd gotten out of bed, he headed to the police station. Mac's truck was out front, indicating he was here. Mac was the only person Ty could talk to about this.

Ty walked inside just as Mac stepped from his office.

Mac stopped in his tracks and flinched. "You look like you've been run over."

"I feel like I have. Can we talk?"

"Of course. Come into my office. The FBI just left. I've been up all night dealing with them. The good news is that they're keeping what happened quiet."

"Islanders will ask questions, though. They'll know something was up."

"They will. But we've got our story in place. Everyone thinks Cassidy's old boyfriend died a month ago when he came into town. Now they'll think her boyfriend's brother came here to exact revenge for his death."

"And Ryan's presence in town? How do we explain that?"

"We don't. We tell people he was an investor looking to buy some property, and you tried to convince him to invest in Hope House."

"Let's hope people fall for it."

Mac closed his door to the office and pointed to a chair in the corner. "Have a seat."

Ty didn't bother to argue. He plopped down, his body both weary and wired at the same time. As Mac thrust some coffee from a nearby carafe into his hand, Ty muttered, "Thanks."

"You're welcome." Mac leaned against his desk. "Now, what's going on?"

"Ryan and one of his sidekicks are headed to Atlanta," Ty said. "They're going to kill Cassidy, Mac."

"How do you know that?"

Ty explained to him what he'd done.

Mac grunted and nodded as he comprehended Ty's words. "What do you want to do?"

"I want to go to Atlanta. I want to warn Cassidy. I want to keep her safe." He fisted his hands as he said the words, all the adrenaline inside him putting a fire in his blood.

Mac leaned back and laced his fingers together in thought. "Did you try and call Cassidy?"

Ty nodded slowly. "She must have left her phone here. It goes right to voice mail."

Mac grunted again. "But she asked you to stay? To let her go?"

"That's right. But I don't know if Cassidy knows what she's walking into." Ty paused and raked a hand through his hair. "I don't know what to do. I want to help her. But I also want to respect her wishes."

"But that guy said he was going to kill her?"

"That's right." The fire blazed hotter at the thought of anyone hurting his girl.

After a moment of quiet contemplation, Mac's gaze met his. "You should go. Even if you betray her trust, at least she'll be alive. Once you get there, you can always hang back if it seems like she's got a handle on things."

Ty released his breath, relieved to hear that Mac agreed with him. He'd been hoping for some confirmation. He didn't need to hear it. He could make the decision on his own.

But his emotions were so involved that he didn't want to risk doing something that might put Cassidy in danger.

"Thanks, Mac." Ty stood. "I just needed some feedback."

Mac stood also and grabbed his keys. "When do we leave?"

"You're going?" Had Ty heard him correctly?

"Of course. I think of Cassidy as a daughter."

"It would be nice to have someone as backup."

Mac nodded toward the door and took a step forward. "Then let's hit the road."

Cassidy stared out the window of her hotel room, watching as the rain drizzled down the thick, expansive window.

Her gaze focused on a lone drop that hit the glass and then ran downward.

She felt like that drop. Isolated. Alone. Going down.

Her thoughts were over the top, and Cassidy knew it. She did. But that didn't stop her contemplation.

She kept replaying, over and over again, what had happened yesterday.

Cassidy had come close to losing her life. Close to losing everything.

Her ribs still ached. The bandage around her midsection was tight and made it hard to breathe. Her eye was swollen. Her lip was busted. One of her teeth hurt also, probably from being punched.

"How are you this morning?" Samuel emerged from his bedroom, already dressed and ready to go for the day.

He sat in the chair across from her, his concerned eyes on her. He'd shaved and looked more like the

Samuel Cassidy knew: more professional and less rough.

"As to be expected."

"You ready to do this?" Samuel straightened the legs of his khaki pants, but his intense gaze remained on her.

Ending this was all she could think about. "Hopefully Ryan will follow our breadcrumbs and show up here."

And then they would stop all this once and for all.

"The plan is risky," Samuel said.

Cassidy knew that more than anyone. "It's the only way."

Samuel nodded slowly. "As long as you're sure. It's your life on the line."

"Greater love has no man than to lay down his life."

"Or her life."

Cassidy smiled sadly and stood. "Or hers. Let me get ready. Then let's go."

Cassidy donned a long brown wig. Professional attire. She'd covered up her injuries with some makeup.

And then she looked in the mirror.

The ghost of someone Cassidy once knew stared back.

Cady Matthews.

She blanched at the image. So put together. Even a glimmer of that driven, ambitious woman seemed to reappear in her gaze.

But this wasn't who Cassidy—Cady—was anymore.

No, the last few months had changed her—for the better.

But, for now, this look and donning her old self was necessary.

She and Samuel headed outside on the busy city streets of downtown Atlanta. At eleven o'clock, she stepped into Jitters, a coffee shop that smelled every bit like a coffee shop should. Not just like coffee, but like hazelnut and cinnamon and chocolate.

The scent made her miss Seattle for a minute.

Her gaze traveled the room before stopping on a familiar face.

Deanna Mars. A member of Cassidy's college sorority and current news anchor for BNN, a national cable news network. The woman looked the same. Neat blonde hair. Perfectly applied makeup. A trim figure that gave a nod to her former women's volleyball champion status.

Meeting Deanna was risky. But Cassidy hoped it would be worth it.

"Cady?" Deanna stood from the table.

Cassidy leaned forward and gave her old friend an air kiss. "It's me."

"It's been a long time. You look great."

Cassidy sat across from her. "You too. A news anchor, huh? Impressive. I loved that interview you did with the British prime minister several months ago."

Deanna beamed. "Thanks. I feel incredibly lucky. I'm married with two kids, and I'm working my dream job."

"Couldn't have happened to a nicer person."

A waitress came and brought them coffee. Deanna explained that she'd ordered for Cassidy and hoped she still liked her coffee with a splash of cream and two sugars.

She did.

Deanna's expression morphed from friendly to serious, and the air around them seemed to change. "You said you had something serious to share with me. What's going on?"

Cassidy took a deep breath. This was it. Her plan. Part of it, at least.

And once she set this in motion, there was no turning back.

"I need to tell you something that just might be one of the biggest news stories of your career," Cassidy started.

And then she told Deanna. About being undercover. About Ryan Samson. About the hit on her life. She left out the information about Lantern Beach and her time there, however.

There were some things Deanna shouldn't know.

"Those are some pretty big accusations," Deanna said when Cassidy had finished. Her coffee appeared to be forgotten, and her instincts as a reporter were raging —salivating—for a good story. DH-7 was one of the hottest topics in the country.

"I know." Cassidy played with the handle of her own coffee mug, praying this risk paid off.

"You really want to come forward with what you told me?"

Do I? Cassidy already knew the answer. "I do. I've been in hiding for a while. But I'll only do the interview tomorrow, and I'll only do it live."

Deanna blanched. "That doesn't give me much time."

"I know. But if I don't do it tomorrow, I might die before I can tell my story."

Deana let out a breath. "This is serious, isn't it? Like life-or-death serious?"

"Unfortunately, yes."

Deanna leaned back and nodded. "I'll see what I can do. I have to talk to my boss. I wish it was that simple and easy, but there's a process we have to go through before things go on the air. We have to fact-check."

"I totally understand that, and I have evidence that will make it easier for you. But my offer still stands as it is, and you don't get the information until I get a confirmation. I can only do it tomorrow. After that, I'll either be dead or I'll be somewhere off-grid and unreachable. I'm sorry to put you in this position."

"I get it. I do. I'll get back in touch with you later today, okay?"

Cassidy released the breath that she'd been holding. "That sounds great. Thank you."

She was going public with this story. And, if her plan worked, Ryan would be going away for life.

CHAPTER
TWENTY-FIVE

CASSIDY GOT the call that evening. The call from Deanna. Her old friend had called several times before that, begging Cassidy to change her timeline and her terms.

She'd refused.

But finally Deanna said her producer had approved the story *and* the timeline.

From the safety of her hotel room, Cassidy did a pre-interview. She repeated her story to Deanna, but this time it was recorded. She offered the information she knew, and emailed Deanna copies of key documents from the jump drive that Ryan was so desperate to get his hands on.

Even if Ryan ended up killing her, he'd still be sunk.

And that was exactly what Cassidy needed to know.

She hung up after confirming the details for tomorrow's meeting.

"It looks like everything is falling into place," Samuel told her.

Cassidy leaned back on the couch and nodded. "I guess it is."

"It's still not too late to back out. To run. To hide again. Maybe on a Caribbean island this time."

"There's only one island for me." The one where Ty was. She'd told him once that anywhere with him felt like home, and she'd meant those words.

"Okay then. We should go over our plan. I've already talked to the FBI. We have four agents who will be working with us to ensure you're safe."

"Got it."

"We also need to talk about backup plans. By now, Ryan probably knows where you are. BNN is advertising your upcoming interview. So this is how it's going to go down tomorrow . . ." Samuel started. "If we miss one of these details, our whole plan could be ruined."

Ty had driven most of the way to Atlanta, stopping only for gas, food, and the restroom. Mac had grabbed a few minutes of shut-eye as they traveled. At eleven p.m., they stopped on the outskirts of town.

Now that they were close, Ty's adrenaline had surged again.

He wanted to find Cassidy. He wanted answers. Unfortunately, it wasn't that easy.

Instead, he and Mac were now grabbing some dinner at an overpriced joint attached to the lobby of their hotel.

Normally, Ty might enjoy the burger and fries. But right now nothing tasted good.

Mac absently munched on a french fry and stared at his phone. "He's here. In Atlanta."

Ty nodded. Mac had been able to trace the phone number of the man Ty had talked to—the one who said he was going to kill Cassidy. The phone number itself was associated with a track phone, so they didn't know who was on the other end of the line. No doubt it was someone Ryan had hired to do his dirty work.

"At least we're still on track," Ty said. "However, that doesn't make me feel better."

"We know Cassidy is here. We just don't know where. You're right—I can't track her number, which means she was smart enough to take the battery out."

"The question is: have Ryan and his sidekick found her?"

"That is the question of the hour," Mac said. "We have no way of knowing that yet. I'd say you could call this guy back, but by now he's got to know that wasn't Ryan he talked to."

"And if he was smart, he didn't mention that fact to Ryan."

A bad feeling loomed in Ty's gut.

He didn't like this. Not at all.

Mac nudged him and nodded toward a TV playing in the corner of the restaurant. "Listen."

The newscaster's voice sounded across the room. "And stay tuned tomorrow for an exclusive interview with Cady Matthews, a woman who went undercover with one of the world's most dangerous gangs."

Ty sucked in a breath and stood, moving closer so he could hear better.

"Matthews claims to have evidence that can bring the whole organization down—and she has surprising information on who is calling the shots," the female anchor said. "Tune in tomorrow morning at ten to hear her story."

"What are you thinking, Cassidy?" Ty muttered.

Was that her plan? To go live with her story? Did she think that would keep her alive?

No, it would just expose her.

They didn't have time to eat, Ty realized. They needed to find Cassidy.

Now.

TWENTY-SIX

23 WEEKS EARLIER

BACK UP IN the room she shared with three other women, Cady stared at the space she'd called home for the past two months.

She wouldn't miss this one bit.

She only had a brief window in which she could leave. Raul was gone on whatever trip he was taking out of town. His core group of minions were brokering some kind of deal twenty minutes away. Everyone else was either high or partying.

Now was the time to do this.

She'd even called Samuel and told him about her plan. He was going to send someone to pick her up at the end of the street. At this point, it didn't matter anymore if someone saw her get into the police car. No, all that mattered was that she got away.

Because when they discovered she was the narc, she'd be dead.

It would be her heart that Raul was showing people as an example next time.

She shuddered at the thought of it.

Cady didn't have any more time to waste.

The good news was that she knew, no matter what happened, she'd done the right thing. Her life might never be normal again. No, this had irreversibly changed her. It showed her a side of life she never wanted to experience again.

And now it was time to go.

She shut the door behind her.

The hallway was empty.

Good.

She left everything behind—even her purse. There was nothing from this life that she wanted to take with her. Nothing at all.

Keeping her steps even, she started down the corridor.

Still no one.

She went into the stairway.

Empty.

And hurried down three flights.

At the bottom, she paused.

She was almost home free now. Almost to the point of walking away and never looking back. Just a few more steps, and she'd be there.

A burst of joy exploded in her heart.

She stepped from the stairwell.

The building seemed eerily quiet.

Which made this the perfect time.

Without looking back, she pushed through the squeaky doorway and stepped into the alley outside.

She was done with this assignment, once and for all.

CHAPTER
TWENTY-SEVEN

TODAY'S GOALS: FINISH THIS.
MAKE SURE RYAN GETS WHAT
HE DESERVES. PUT THIS ALL
BEHIND ME.

CASSIDY STARED at herself in the mirror again and adjusted the business suit she wore.

She was going to do this interview with Deanna. It was the only way out.

"It's not too late to turn back," Samuel said.

"I know. But I'm in this. All the way."

Samuel offered a curt nod, as if he knew he wouldn't change her mind and had resigned himself to that fact. "Then let's go. We'll review things on the way."

That was right. It was a live interview. Well-advertised.

Ryan should be crawling out of his skin right about now.

Good.

Before they reached the door of the hotel room, Cassidy grabbed Samuel's arm. There was something she needed to say to him before they left. Before the first domino was tapped, sending the rest into an unstoppable cascade.

"Samuel, if this goes wrong, there are things I need you to tell Ty."

"Things won't go wrong."

She pressed her lips together, knowing he was being optimistic, but that the situation was serious. "Please, Samuel. I need you to promise me."

He stared at her a moment before nodding. "Okay. I promise. I'll tell him what our plan was. But we've got to believe this is going to work."

"Thank you." She felt better knowing that if things went terribly wrong, at least Ty would have some closure.

Samuel drove her to the station, and they pulled into the parking garage beside a high-rise building in downtown Atlanta.

Cassidy's hands trembled as she got out of the car.

Please, Lord. I need Your grace right now. More than ever. Your favor. Your courage. And anything else You can give me.

As she closed her door, she heard a sound in the distance and paused.

It sounded like an . . . ice cream truck.

And it was playing "Battle Hymn of the Republic."

Hearing it made her think of Elsa, and she smiled.

"Probably just a food truck," Samuel muttered.

Of course. Cassidy's ice cream truck hadn't followed her here to Atlanta. Cassidy didn't share any kind of intrinsic connection with the truck, even if it sometimes felt like she did.

Samuel put a hand on her elbow, jarring her back to reality. Cassidy glanced around, trying not to show her nerves, even though she felt like they were screaming for all to see and hear.

This was it.

The moment it all boiled down to. The moment that would make or break her.

"We're a little early," Cassidy muttered.

"I know. Traffic wasn't as heavy as I anticipated."

"I hope it doesn't mess anything up."

"Let's get to the stairway and get you over to the station," Samuel said. "You should have let me drop you off."

She couldn't risk being alone. Not even for a moment. Even if the FBI agents were on backup.

They hurried across the cement floor, their footsteps echoing in the hollow space.

She felt jumpier than a tick as she walked. Her head pounded in anticipation of what was about to happen.

She only hoped her plan worked.

Please, Lord . . .

"You should have let him drop you off, Cady," someone said in the distance. "I thought you'd be smarter than this."

She froze, and the hair on her arms rose.

Before she could react, Samuel reached for his gun.

It was too late.

A bullet rushed through the air, hitting Samuel in the arm. His gun flew out of his hands.

Cassidy gasped. "Samuel! Are you okay?"

His face squeezed with pain.

Cassidy's gaze traveled across the pavement. Samuel's gun. Just as she lunged toward the weapon, Ryan stepped forward. His foot covered it.

"I wouldn't do that if I were you," Ryan said.

Cassidy glanced up. Studied Ryan a moment. He didn't look like the consummate professional she once knew. No, he wore ratty jeans and a black T-shirt. Even his voice seemed to change from a cultured politician to a street-smart kid. The transformation amazed her, and almost made Cassidy forget her mission here.

On her other side, another person appeared.

Ricky Ernest. The PI her parents had hired. Someone she'd briefly dated.

He no longer looked like the preppy boy who played football for the college team. No, time hadn't been good to him. He'd probably gained thirty pounds. His hairline was receding. His skin looked looser, baggier.

What had happened to him in the years since they'd last spoken?

She didn't have time to find out now, nor did she care to hear his story. She had no compassion for anyone who worked for Ryan.

"Et tu, Brute?" she muttered.

Ricky shrugged. "The paycheck was too good to pass up."

Cassidy didn't have time to argue with him. "People could come through here at any minute. You really didn't think out this plan, did you?"

Ryan smiled, and Cassidy knew there was more to this.

"Actually, we blocked the one and only entrance to this garage with a wayward ice cream truck." Ryan smiled more broadly. "I thought you might appreciate the sentiment."

"So that's what the noise is." Clever. Unfortunately clever. "But there's still the stairway."

"You don't think we thought of that too? We knew you were coming here. This is where you park to get into the building. We did fear that Samuel could drop you off, but we had a plan for that also. We covered all the bases. We jimmied each of the doors in the stairway. No one is getting up or down."

The blood left her face. This had been a bad idea.

She wished for a moment that she could turn back time. That she could talk herself out of this. That she might have just gone into hiding again.

"Why are you guys doing this?" Her voice shook as she asked the question.

"Shut up!" Ryan barked, aiming his gun at Samuel. "One wrong move, and your buddy dies. I'm pretty much over you right now, Cady. Actually, I have been for a long time."

Hardly able to breathe, she listened to Ryan, not daring to argue. Her heart pounded so loudly, she felt sure everyone could hear it. Why had she ever thought this was a good idea? That she was going to get away with it?

All she could do right now was try to buy more time.

Cassidy inched away. "You had all those women killed. The ones who looked like me. You put a bounty on my head."

Ryan scowled. "I can't let you ruin everything."

"And you chose me on purpose, didn't you?" Cassidy continued, still inching backward. "Because you want money from my father. You want revenge."

"You know it. And we want more than money and revenge. We want to bend his ear. We need his influence."

"All for some stupid drug?"

"That drug is making us millions. Between money and being elected into office, the world is at my fingertips." Ryan raised his gun. "And don't move another inch! You don't think I see you?"

She froze, yet her blood seemed to boil.

"I hope it's all worth it when your soul burns in hell." Her voice sounded more biting than she'd intended.

"Oh, it will be." Ryan smiled in a way that reminded her of the soulless look Raul always had in his eyes.

How could Cassidy not have seen this earlier? The clues had been right in front of her face. Yet Ryan had pulled the wool over everyone's eyes, not just Cassidy's. The people who worked with him in the prosecuting attorney's office. The public who'd elected him into office. Even Cassidy's family.

"You're not doing that interview," Ryan continued. "I don't know what you were thinking, but there's no way you're going on air. Besides, no one will believe you."

"Because everyone thinks you're a saint?"

That evil gleam returned to his eyes. "Everyone *knows* I'm a saint. The savior to the city—soon the state. I'll move on from there. You're going to have an unfortunate confrontation with someone from DH-7. The fall guy is already in place. And I've already engineered some emails between you and Samuel that will debunk anything you've already told this news anchor."

"What are those emails going to say?" Samuel asked through gritted teeth. He still stood, but one hand grasped his shoulder where blood seeped out.

"It will make it clear that Cady didn't like living in her dad's shadow so she covertly joined DH-7 and you discovered it. It will detail how she's been behind several of the crimes committed. Believe me when I say these emails are convincing."

Cassidy's lip twitched upward in disgust. "You're sick and twisted, I'll give you that. I would have never guessed you to be the leader of DH-7. And to think you're the one who's supposedly prosecuting them. What a joke."

"You're talking too much. We need to get this over with." Ryan raised his gun.

She swallowed hard. "You're going to shoot me?"

"It's the only way to end this. Sorry, babe."

"You really think you're going to get away with this?" Cassidy said. "That there aren't security cameras?"

"We've already taken care of those. I'll walk away, and no one will ever know what happened."

"You've always been clever."

He raised his gun. "Now, let's get this over with."

This was a bad idea, she realized. Cassidy should have thought it through more.

But now it was too late. Entirely too late.

———

Ty stared at the tracking program on his laptop as Mac drove down the road. Mac had managed to trace the phone number that Ty had called earlier, and they were able to see in real time where the device was.

However, the program had gone down last night, leaving Mac and Ty unable to do anything but wait. They'd taken turns, one sleeping while the other watched the computer. Finally, at five a.m., it came back online.

And it was just as Ty feared.

Whoever owned that phone was now right outside the TV station where Cassidy was supposed to go on the air.

"We're almost there," Mac said, speeding around cars.

But traffic was heavy. It was rush hour.

Ty wanted to climb from the truck and race toward the station himself. But he knew that wouldn't get him there any faster.

Finally, they reached the parking garage.

"It looks like he's in there," Ty said, staring at the screen.

Mac jerked to a stop at the entryway. An ice cream truck was there, music blaring. On the other side was a police car, and a bewildered-looking officer inspected the vehicle.

Both of them had effectively blocked the entrance.

"We need to find another way." Mac pulled over to the side of the road and put his truck in park. "I know I'm not supposed to park here, and I'll probably get towed and fined. But I'm doing it anyway."

Ty didn't argue. He jumped out and ran toward the parking garage. When he got to a side door and pulled it, the door didn't budge. "What . . . ?"

Mac tried also, to no avail. "Someone must have jammed it."

Wasting no more time, Ty ran to the cement barrier that separated the first level from the outside world. He hurdled it. Mac climbed over behind him.

"This body isn't what it used to be," he muttered.

Ty glanced around, looking for a sign of anything suspicious. He saw nothing.

Mac put a finger to his lips. "Did you hear that?"

Ty listened. It sounded like someone arguing. Above them.

"Let's go," he said.

He darted to the stairway and pulled the door there. It was also jammed.

The bad feeling in his gut grew stronger.

Someone had planned this.

"We're going to have to run up these levels," Mac said.

"Let's not waste any more time." Ty darted toward the next level.

It was empty.

His muscles tightened, and his pulse pounded as he continued upward.

The third level was empty also.

And the fourth.

But the voices were louder. He had to be almost there.

Now, let's get this over with, someone said in the distance.

Ty's pulse heightened.

He paused as he rounded the corner.

Ryan had a gun to someone's head. A woman with dark hair.

He squinted.

No, that was . . . Cassidy?

Samuel stood not far from her, holding his bleeding shoulder.

Ryan's sidekick heard them and turned his gun toward Ty.

"One more step and I'll shoot," the man yelled.

Ty stopped and raised his hands.

His gaze went to Cassidy. Her eyes widened with surprise, just as her face paled.

She wasn't expecting to see him.

And it appeared Ty was too late.

Mac was just far enough behind him that he wouldn't be much help.

"You should have never gone public with this," Ryan said, venom dripping from his words.

"You left me no choice," Cassidy said.

"No, now I'm leaving you no choice."

Cassidy looked over at Ty, and she mouthed, "I'm sorry."

As her last word slipped out, Ryan pulled the trigger.

Blood covered her chest near her heart.

And she fell to the floor.

CHAPTER
TWENTY-EIGHT

A SOUND LEFT Ty's lips, a noise from deep in his gut like nothing he'd ever heard before. A cry. A scream. A yell. He didn't know which.

Nausea pooled in his gut.

Men in FBI vests flooded the area. Ty had no idea where they'd come from. Right now, he didn't care.

"Help me!" Ryan yelled. "That woman tried to kill me. My bodyguard shot her. He had no choice."

Ty darted toward the scene, but an FBI agent grabbed him. Held him back.

Ty couldn't pull his eyes away from Cassidy's limp body.

She laid on the filthy pavement. Blood continued to cover her chest. Growing.

And she wasn't moving.

Two other FBI agents grabbed Ryan and Ricky. Both of them still rambled, trying to sound like victims.

More commotion sounded behind him. He didn't

even care what it was. From the periphery of his vision, he saw a camera crew bust through a door in the distance and rush inside, filming all of this. They were trailed by Deanna Mars, the anchor of BNN News.

She screamed when she saw Cassidy, and an FBI agent caught the woman as her legs buckled.

Samuel knelt beside Cassidy, still holding his bloody shoulder. He put his finger to her neck. Waited. Frowned.

His gaze met Ty's, and he shook his head.

Mac put his arm around him. "I'm sorry, Ty."

Ty's eyes went to Ryan, and he started to lunge for him. Mac and the FBI agent held him back.

"I need to see her for myself."

Samuel rose, grief etched on his face. "There will be time for that later. Right now, we've got to preserve this crime scene."

"Cassidy . . ."

Samuel locked gazes with him. "I'm sorry, Ty. There are a few things Cassidy wanted me to explain to you in case this happened. But we'll need to go somewhere private."

As Ty stood there in the garage, the ache remained in his heart. Every time he closed his eyes, he saw Cassidy. He heard her muttering that she was sorry.

All the dreams he had for them . . . they dissipated

like the morning fog and left him feeling parched. Life-less. Empty.

It didn't seem real.

Why would Cassidy have put herself in that situation? She was smarter than that.

Did she feel like she didn't have a choice? Like the only way out was to confront this head on?

None of it made sense.

Mac's hand came down on his back. "I'm really sorry, Ty."

"It's going to take a while for me to comprehend this." His eyes filled with tears as the ache in his chest grew.

The coroner carried Cassidy away on a gurney.

The pain in his heart pierced him over and over again.

This couldn't have just happened. It couldn't have. It just wasn't possible.

"I'd like to take you somewhere to talk privately," Samuel said. He'd been bandaged up. Even though there was still blood on his shirt and jacket—and he looked terrible—paramedics had deemed him okay.

Ty nodded, ready to get out of there and away from this craziness.

"The news is already reporting what happened," Samuel said as they walked toward his car.

"Did they report that Cassidy had died?"

"They reported a casualty, but they won't release her name until family has been notified."

"What about Ryan?"

"He's been arrested," Samuel said. "Cassidy was wearing a wire. Ryan will be going away for a long time."

"Was that her end game?" Ty asked.

"You could say that."

They climbed into Samuel's car, and another FBI agent slid behind the wheel. Thirty minutes later, they arrived at the local FBI field office. Samuel led them down a maze of hallways and into a small room with a table and several chairs around it.

"First, I want to let you know how brave Cassidy is—a true hero, even if she never gets the recognition."

More images of Ty's time in the Middle East filled him. He'd given this same talk to the families of his fallen comrades.

A dull ache spread over his heart.

"Why would she have done this?" Ty asked. "I just don't understand. She's smarter than this. She had to know what she was setting herself up for."

Samuel's lips pulled downward. "You're right. She did."

Ty stared at him. "What does that mean?"

Samuel nodded toward the door. The next instant, it opened.

And Cassidy stepped through.

TWENTY-NINE

TEARS welled in Cassidy's eyes when she saw Ty sitting there at the table, his face ashen with grief.

He stood, emotions flashing through his gaze. Grief. Confusion. Joy.

Without wasting any more time, she flew into his arms and held him so tight she could hardly breathe. Her rib cage ached. Her chest hurt from where the bullet had hit her bullet-proof vest.

And she didn't care how much pain she was in.

"You weren't supposed to be there," she whispered.

"Oh, Cassidy . . . you're alive." The gut-wrenching relief in his voice made a new round of tears fill her eyes.

She pulled back so she could look at his face, see his gaze, express with her eyes the things her words could never say.

"I'm so sorry," she said. "I had to be certain everyone really believed I was dead."

"That's what you said right before Ryan shot you." His gaze flickered as he studied her, as he searched for answers.

"Maybe we should sit down."

"I'll give you two a minute," Samuel said.

Cassidy sat down beside Ty—close to him. She never wanted to be far away again. Never wanted to see that kind of trauma in his gaze.

"Maybe you should start at the beginning," Ty said. "Because I obviously have a lot to comprehend right now."

She swallowed hard and glanced at her hands, trying to find the words. Everything seemed surreal and overwhelming and . . . almost like an out-of-body experience, in some ways.

"I didn't want to run for the rest of my life, Ty," she started. "I knew I needed to do something to put an end to all of this. Otherwise, Ryan was going to kill me before the trial ever started."

He nodded and waited for her to continue.

"I also knew whatever my plan was, I needed it to take place far away from Lantern Beach. I didn't want to ever lead anyone back there. That's why I came to Atlanta. It was far enough away."

"I can understand that."

She grabbed his hand and squeezed, wishing she never had to let go. Maybe after today, she wouldn't have to.

She licked her lips and grabbed a remote. She turned

the TV on where a report was playing. Deanna reported on Ryan's arrest. On Cady's death.

Which meant her parents had been updated.

"As far as the world knows, Cady Matthews is dead," she said.

Realization spread across his face. "Which means you're free to live as Cassidy Livingston."

She smiled at his words. "That's right."

"On Lantern Beach?"

"If everything stays according to plan, no one should ever know I was Cady Matthews."

"What about the law enforcement who showed up at the scene at the cottage? Where Greg died?"

"It was limited to a pool of about six FBI agents. Samuel will feed them the story we want them to have and swear them to secrecy on the rest."

"What about the trial?"

"I was wearing a wire, so I recorded everything Ryan said," she shared. "With the leader of DH-7 behind bars, the information that I stole from the gang's headquarters now in the right hands, and Raul dead, DH-7 is expected to fracture and disappear."

Ty leaned closer. "But Cassidy, I saw you get shot."

She rolled her shoulder, still feeling the impact of the bullet. She'd be sore for at least a week. "I was wearing a vest, and I put a fake blood packet beneath my shirt. I knew as soon as it was punctured, it would look like I'd been shot. I figured it would all go down at the news station, which would mean the camera crews would be close by to record everything. They got an anonymous tip."

"You really thought this through, didn't you?"

She shrugged, another ache reminding her of what she'd done. "I didn't have much time. I only knew that faking my death was the only way out of this. I also knew I had to get the truth out there. That's why I went to the news station and why I wore the wire."

Ty dropped his head. "When I thought you were dead . . ."

Cassidy rested her hand on the side of his face. "I know. Believe me, I know. You weren't supposed to show up. After it all happened, Samuel was going to call you. Why did you come?"

"I managed to find Ryan's phone in his rental car, and I called one of the numbers listed there. The guy—Ricky Ernest—thought I was Ryan. He asked if they should stick to the plan—the plan being to kill you. I knew I had to warn you. I knew also that you'd said I should trust you and stay there, but I couldn't let you die."

A smile tugged at her lips. "I should have known."

He pressed his lips against hers. "I love you, Cassidy."

"I love you too, Ty. Always."

"When can you get back to Lantern Beach?"

"Samuel said I may need to stay here a few days before they can get me out of here. Why?"

"Because we're getting married. I thought we talked about this."

She smiled again and pulled a necklace from beneath her shirt. Her ring was there, kept safe. She took it off the chain and slipped it back onto her finger. "I'd like that. Very much."

Ty and Cassidy sat across from each other at the safe house where Cassidy was staying until Samuel confirmed it was safe to leave.

Ty had taken it upon himself to be her personal guardian, and he hadn't left her side except to sleep.

It had been three days since Cassidy had supposedly died. Three days since this nightmare ended. Three days since Cassidy took the first step in regaining the life she'd always dreamed about.

An FBI agent outside the door opened it, and Samuel came inside. He sat across from them, placing some coffee and muffins on the table. His shoulder was bandaged, but thankfully the bullet had only grazed his skin. It could have been much worse.

"Good morning," he said.

"You have an update?" Cassidy grabbed a cup but didn't have the stomach to take a sip yet.

She'd been anxiously waiting to hear about any new developments. The past three days had been wonderful —being with Ty. Knowing this was over. Anticipating the future.

But she'd also felt anxious for finality.

"I do have some updates for you," Samuel said.

"First of all, our original plan worked. Everyone on Lantern Beach thinks your crazy ex-boyfriend's brother came into town and tried to kill you. They think you're in the hospital right now, but that you're okay."

She nodded, hating to deceive people. But, in this case, how could she not?

"We talked to the innkeeper—casually," Samuel continued. "She believes Ryan is your ex's brother, and that he came up here from Florida. We made up a story about how your new Navy SEAL boyfriend saved you, and that was all it took to distract her from what had really happened. She's apparently a total romantic."

Cassidy exchanged a smile with Ty.

"Ryan knows there's no way for him to win this. There's too much evidence against him. He's been slow at giving up information, but he's trying to cut a deal. Otherwise, he knows he'll be killed in prison. He wants solitary confinement somewhere he has a chance for survival."

"I hate to say it, but he deserves anything he gets at this point," Cassidy said. "There's nothing in me that feels sorry for him."

"I agree. But I thought you'd want to know that he did confess that his uncle killed your friend Lucy. Your theory was right. They'd blackmailed Lucy's father, Hiroto, into creating new and improved versions of flakka over the years. Lucy's mom was supposed to die that evening. Apparently, Hiroto had refused to create anything else for them and threatened to walk away. They decided to teach him a lesson."

Cassidy's heart pounded with a wave of grief. "At least there are answers now. That's all I ever wanted."

"What about the trial?" Ty asked. "Since Cady Matthews is dead, that means Cassidy is out of this, right?"

"That's right. With the information she gathered while undercover, as well as the recording of Ryan's confession, we have enough to prosecute him without revealing that Cady is still alive. She's free to live the rest of her life as Cassidy Livingston. Or Cassidy Chambers." Samuel smiled.

Cassidy and Ty exchanged a look.

She liked the sound of that. Based on Ty's smile, he did too.

"What about my parents, Samuel?" Cassidy asked. "What will we tell them?"

"Actually, your parents heard what happened. They're on their way."

"Here?" She sat up straight. "What are you going to tell them?"

"I thought you might want to at least tell them goodbye. But it's your choice."

"They don't know I'm not actually dead?" Cassidy asked.

"We haven't told them the truth yet. But we're going to let that be your choice."

She sat back, feeling numb as she thought it through. "I guess I'll talk to them."

"Okay then. I'll arrange it."

Two hours later, Samuel returned—with her mom

and dad. Cassidy held her breath as her parents stepped inside, both looking as prim and proper as ever. Her mom wore a tailored sheath dress. Her dad in a neatly pressed shirt and crisp slacks.

She stared at them a moment, unsure how to greet them.

Her mom let out a little cry and pulled Cassidy into her arms. "I've never been so happy to see you."

Cassidy held her mom, drinking in her expensive perfume. She thought it would turn her stomach, but it brought her a strange comfort instead.

As soon as her mother pulled away, her dad enveloped Cassidy in his embrace. His skinny arms wrapped around her. "I've missed you, Cady."

"I've missed you too, Dad." And she meant the words as she said them.

Which surprised even her, considering how absent her parents had been for most of her life. But they were still her parents.

"I'm proud of you, Cady," her dad said. "Agent Stephens told us how brave you were and about everything you did. He also told us that we have to pretend you didn't survive."

"Only if you want me to actually survive."

Her dad offered a sad smile. "We do."

Cassidy remembered that Ty was behind her and stepped back. "Oh, Mom, Dad. This is Ty. I'm sorry."

They shook hands.

"He's my neighbor. A former Navy SEAL. And the

man I'm going to marry." She held her breath, waiting for her parents to rain down their judgment.

Instead they nodded. "We're glad you found someone," her mom said.

"You promise to take care of her?" Dad asked.

Ty nodded. "I promise."

Cassidy extended her arm behind her toward the table. "Why don't we sit down, have some coffee and catch up?"

Samuel called her over to the door a moment and lowered his voice. "You can go back in two days to Lantern Beach. We'll escort you there. And you never have to hear from us again, Cassidy."

She nodded, feeling another chapter in her life closing. "It's been quite the ride, hasn't it?"

"It sure has. I look forward to seeing what new things there are in store for you."

LISA AND SKYE stepped back and stared at Cassidy as she stood in the living room of her cottage. A full-length mirror had been set up in the corner. Flowers decorated the space. The mild day outside drifted in through the open windows.

"You look gorgeous," Lisa said with a confident nod. "Ty's jaw is going to drop."

Cassidy looked in the mirror and smiled. She'd gotten a second-hand wedding gown at a shop here in town. It was simple with a sweetheart neckline and a shirred bodice that nipped at the waist, creating a soft silhouette. Skye had made a veil for her, and it was also simple—just a few sheets of lace that hung at the top of a long, loose bun Cassidy wore at the nape of her neck.

For flowers, she carried a bouquet of oriental lilies. They'd been Lucy's favorite, and it seemed only appropriate to honor her friend today. Especially after all they'd been through—even if part of that bond had happened after Lucy's death.

Live like today is your last day on earth.

The advice from her friend's Day-at-a-Glance had been echoing in Cassidy's mind for the past week. She was finally doing it. She was taking life by the horns, and nothing was going to get in her way this time.

Thank You, God, for finally opening my eyes to what's important—faith, family, friends. Help me not to squander this opportunity.

"Where's the honeymoon going to be?" Skye asked.

"I don't know. Ty said he plans to surprise me." Ty and Samuel had coordinated something together since Cassidy still needed to remain low-key for a while. "I have the impression it has something to do with a boat and miles and miles of endless water in the middle of nowhere."

Someone knocked at the door. Cassidy turned and saw Del standing there with a wide grin on her face, and a new curly red wig atop her head.

Warmth spread through Cassidy at the sight.

Cassidy rushed toward the woman and wrapped her arms around her. Del's doctor had approved her and her husband, Frank, to fly out to Lantern Beach for the ceremony.

"I'm so glad you made it," Cassidy murmured in Del's ear, still holding her close. "It means the world to us."

"I wouldn't have missed it for anything. Especially

not for cancer. The disease has already stolen too much from me. No more."

Cassidy pulled back, feeling the tears glistening in her eyes. "But you're feeling okay?"

"It's too soon to say for sure that I'll be okay, but my doctor feels the prognosis is really good."

"Nothing could make me happier."

Del grinned—actually, she beamed. "You know what makes me happy? Seeing my boy happy. His father and I are over the moon. You'll make the best daughter-in-law, Cassidy. In fact, could I just think of you as my daughter?"

"I'd love that."

"Then it's a done deal." She stepped back, glancing at Lisa and Skye. "And you both look gorgeous as well."

"Thank you," Lisa and Skye said.

They wore pale yellow sundresses, a simple design they'd be able to wear again. There was no need to waste money on fancy dresses that would only be put into storage.

"Okay, I've got to get back out there," Del said. "I just wanted to say hi."

After she left, Cassidy glanced out the window of her cottage and smiled at the scene outside. There on the sand near the rolling waves of the mighty Atlantic were six rows of white chairs. Ty had built a driftwood pergola near the makeshift stage area, and Lisa and Skye had decorated it with lilies as well.

Carter Denver, the town's local singer/songwriter,

sat in a chair near the front with his guitar. Jack Wilson stood beneath the pergola. He was the new preacher in town, and a chaplain Ty had known while in the military.

All of Cassidy's new friends were seated on the seats there. Friends from church. From around town.

Jimmy James had come, as well as Quinton, Wheezer, Ralph, and even the woman from the inn.

Cassidy's friend Ernestine was here and sat beside Doc Clemson, the town's doctor and medical examiner.

Ty's friends Austin and Wes would be his groomsmen. They'd decided against formal attire, and all the guys wore khakis and white button-up shirts instead.

Kujo waited with a small bag attached to his collar. He was going to be their ring bearer.

After the ceremony, Lisa and her crew would cater the reception. She'd made all their favorite dishes, including grilled cheese with peaches, salt-and-vinegar potato chip cookies, and her newest favorite recipe: cheesesteak egg rolls.

"It's time," Lisa said, glancing at the clock on the wall. "Are you ready?"

Cassidy smiled. "I've been ready."

"We could all see this coming from a mile away," Skye said. "I'm really happy for you."

They all stepped outside and took their places.

Just as Lisa started down the walkway, someone ran down the driveway.

Serena.

She was dressed like someone from *Grease* with an

A-line skirt and some type of scarf tied over her hair. She squealed when she saw Cassidy and threw her arms around her.

"You came," Cassidy said. "All the way from Michigan. I thought you had class."

"I wouldn't have missed this for the world. And, girl, I've got more class than you can imagine."

Cassidy chuckled. "You've got more character than anyone I know. But, really, I didn't know you were coming."

"Coming? I'm staying. I'm going to finish my classes online."

"You're staying here? In Lantern Beach?"

She nodded. "That's right. And I'm buying Elsa from you."

"My ice cream truck?" Cassidy hadn't even put it up for sale—though it was a great idea.

"That's okay, right? And I'm hoping Ty can reverse that little upgrade he did."

"What upgrade?"

"You know, the one where he made sure music no longer randomly plays. Random songs are a big selling point. People on social media talk about Elsa all the time. She's like the Lost Colony of Lantern Beach. We need a little mystery here."

"I'll let you talk to Ty about it later."

"It's a deal. Okay, I've got a ceremony to get to."

As Carter started playing the wedding march, Cassidy joined Mac at the top of the sand dune. He kissed her cheek. "You look beautiful."

"You're just trying to make me blush."

"I'm telling the truth," he said, all glib gone. "You're one special lady, Cassidy."

She actually found herself blushing. "Thank you."

"You ready to take over as police chief?"

That new development had been in the works this week. Mac didn't want the position full time anymore, and he'd insisted that Cassidy should have it. Samuel had helped Cassidy obtain a false PI license.

After talking with the town leaders and explaining that she'd worked for a security firm in the past, they'd agreed to hire Cassidy. Cassidy had only agreed if Mac would stay on as a consultant.

She was going to start in two weeks—after her honeymoon was over. Ty hadn't told her where they were going, and it didn't matter to Cassidy. She just wanted to be with Ty. Now and forever.

Ty's eyes took on a glow like Cassidy had never seen when he spotted her. Her heart felt as if she might burst with happiness.

Before she knew it, it was time for them to say their vows. Ty took Cassidy's hands in his, and she felt them tremble just a bit.

"Cassidy, from the moment I saw you, I knew I'd never be the same."

Cassidy smiled as she remembered their confrontation at a local store after he'd cut her off in traffic. It had been a rocky start, to say the least.

"I knew from the moment I met you that you were the girl for me. I haven't been able to stop thinking about you since then. And I know I never want to lose you. I know life isn't always going to be easy, but I know that it will always be better with you by my side."

Tears sprang to her eyes.

She mouthed, "I love you."

He kissed her hand. "I love you too."

"Hey, you two," Jack said. "No kissing yet. That's not until the end."

All the guests laughed.

"Ty Chambers, as I've told you before, you're my tender warrior." Cassidy's throat tightened at the words. "Anywhere I am with you feels like home. Being here with you in Lantern Beach made me realize what I was lacking in my life. It made me realize what's important, and I'm thrilled to spend my life with you. I wouldn't have it any other way."

They exchanged rings, and Jack prayed over them and their marriage. As soon as Jack said amen, he flashed a wide grin at Cassidy and Ty. "I now pronounce you husband and wife. You may kiss the bride."

Ty's lips met hers, a wonderful promise of what was to come.

Cassidy had found the people she loved and the place where she belonged, and she couldn't wait to make a life here on Lantern Beach. A real life. With Ty. As police chief.

You must first go through fire before you become beautiful.

Day-at-a-Glance wisdom.
And none was ever so true.

~~~

Thank you for reading *Deadly Undertow*. If you enjoyed this book, please consider leaving a review.

Keep reading for an introduction to the next installment of Lantern Beach Universe: Lantern Beach Romantic Suspense
~~~

INTRODUCING LANTERN BEACH ROMANTIC SUSPENSE

Books in the Lantern Beach Romantic Suspense series are standalone and do not need to be read in order. Each features a pulse-pounding story centered around a beloved resident of Lantern Beach.

TIDES OF DECEPTION: CHAPTER ONE

"I understand," Austin Brooks muttered into his phone. "You've given me a lot to think about, and I'll wait for a follow-up call."

Austin hit End on his cell, trying to come to terms with what he'd just learned. But his thoughts staggered inside him, tumultuous and unsettled instead.

He'd just gotten the call he'd been waiting for. So why did unease and regret tug at him? He'd set all of this in motion, so none of it should be a surprise.

This wasn't the time to chew on those thoughts, though. No, his current job needed all his attention.

Austin put the four-wheel-drive vehicle back into Drive. He adjusted his grip on the steering wheel, pushed his sunglasses up higher, and glanced out the window.

The ocean stared back, and it looked as unsettled as his thoughts. Then again, the water always looked angry on Lantern Beach. People didn't call this area of the East Coast the Graveyard of the Atlantic for nothing.

"Was that an update on your secret project?" Skye Lavinia's voice pulled him from his thoughts.

Austin glanced over at her. He'd temporarily forgotten she was on beach-patrol duty with him. Two of the regular rescue crew had gotten food poisoning at a party the night before, and Austin had been called in as a last-minute replacement.

He'd just been recertified, but it had been a long time since he'd lifeguarded. With the influx of crowds they'd had here in Lantern Beach during the off-season, everyone was short-staffed—including beach rescue. Skye was just along for moral support.

His heart skipped a beat when he saw her lithe frame—as it always did when he looked at her.

She was beautiful.

And off-limits.

The walls she kept up around her made that clear, and Austin would be wise to keep it in mind.

He remembered her question, and his phone call echoed in his mind. "Yes, that was about my secret project."

Austin turned back to scan the beachgoers in front of him for a moment. Though it was October, there were still people here on the shores soaking in the unseasonably warm day.

"When are you going to tell me what you're doing?"

Austin shrugged, partly enjoying her interest in his

project, and, in return, her interest in him. He probably enjoyed it more than he should. But Austin wasn't being coy as much as he was cautious when it came to keeping her at arm's length.

"I don't know when I'll spill the beans," he finally said as they bounced over the uneven sand. "Maybe I'll tell *you* what I'm doing as soon as you tell *me* a secret—like why you hate the water so much."

The curiosity slipped from her eyes, and Skye raised her chin teasingly. "By the way, watch out for that lady with the earbuds on. I'm sure she doesn't hear you coming. And, I see you how you are, but I'm not making any deals. We can both just keep our secrets."

And maybe that was their problem. There were too many secrets between them.

Besides, calling it a secret project made the whole thing sound so lighthearted—like Austin was building a bookshelf or starting his own YouTube channel for his woodworking endeavors. But the truth was, Austin's undertaking was really a lot more personal.

And maybe that's what really stopped him from sharing any details with Skye. It would be like sharing a piece of his heart. Once that piece was gone, he might never get it back.

Focus, Austin. Focus. And why are you mentally quoting after-school specials from your childhood?

He grabbed a handful of chocolate-covered raisins from the bag beside him and popped them in his mouth as he skirted around a group of fishermen who chatted while their rods rested in holders in the sand.

No sooner had Austin gone around them did something catch his eye. He pressed the brakes as he spotted something in the water a good twenty yards out. He squinted. Were those hands? Flailing hands?

"What is it?" Concern gripped Skye's features as she leaned toward him.

His heartrate quickened. He jammed the truck in Park, threw his door open, and his feet hit the sand.

"I think there's someone out there in the water." Austin stared at the ocean and squinted when he saw the person again. Someone definitely needed help out there. "Do me a favor—call backup."

Wasting no more time, he stripped off his shirt and grabbed the orange rescue tube from the pickup bed and strapped it across his chest. He abandoned his flip-flops and dashed toward the water.

Maybe the ominous feeling in his gut wasn't a fluke.

Skye held her breath as she watched Austin dive into the turbulent ocean. She watched his strong, powerful strokes as he went against the current, putting his own life on the line to save another. As he battled the waves, her gaze darted beyond Austin. Someone *was* out there —and in trouble.

Oh, Lord, please protect Austin. And protect the person he's trying to save. Don't let the ocean claim an innocent life.

She called for backup. Then, moving in autopilot, she climbed from the beach patrol truck and lumbered toward the raging shoreline. As the wind blew against Skye's face, she raked a hand through her hair, trying to get the strands from her eyes so she could watch the scene unfold.

A small crowd gathered, each person's gaze fixated on the rescue. The beach activities around her seemed to stop—the volleyball game, the boogie boarding, the fishing. Everyone waited to see what would happen.

Skye wrapped her arms across her chest and continued to stare, trying not to anticipate the worst. The ocean was a formidable foe. Skye shuddered whenever she thought about going in those waters.

She wasn't a strong swimmer—and she'd almost lost her life to the ocean once. Ever since then, her throat went dry whenever anyone suggested she go deeper than to her knees in the water.

She pushed aside the memories.

Instead, her heart went into her throat as she waited, as she watched. Austin reached the person and wrapped his arms around the guy's chest, the rescue tube between them. Then, on his back, Austin began swimming toward the shore.

Skye released her breath. Maybe this would all be okay. But Austin still had to make it back to dry land. The waves and the current were strong today, and the swim would be exhausting, even for the most seasoned rescuer.

Dear Lord, watch over them. Please.

Just as paramedics pulled up and rushed toward the crowds, Austin reached the shore. He stood, reached into the water, and carried the victim toward the sand.

The victim was . . . a boy.

That had been a *boy* out there, Skye realized. The child was probably only seven or eight years old, at the most.

Austin placed him on the sand, and the paramedics surrounded the boy, taking over. Skye moved through the crowds until she reached Austin. She studied him for any sign he'd been harmed.

His dark, wavy hair was wet and shoved back from his face. Specks of water still clung to his short, neat beard. He had the hard-earned physique of someone who did both physical labor and took care of himself.

And he appeared to be okay right now.

"You good?" Skye gently touched his arm, wanting to hear the words for herself.

He nodded, still hauling in deep breaths. "Yeah, I'm fine."

"Good job out there." She'd always known he was a hero, but today had only confirmed it.

Austin's gaze didn't leave the boy. "I'm just glad I got to him in time."

The boy . . . he was conscious. Coughing. Lying on the sand.

At least he was awake and breathing.

Thank You, Jesus.

Skye glanced around the windswept landscape. Where were this boy's parents? Why weren't they out here? Worried about him?

Her gaze veered back to the boy. She sucked in a breath when she saw his face. His dark hair. His high cheek bones. The broad set of his eyebrows.

Somehow . . . some reason . . . he looked familiar.

But that was crazy. Unless maybe the boy and his family had come to her produce stand earlier this week. That was probably it.

Yet, if Skye had seen him earlier, she would remember.

His familiarity wasn't because she'd seen him before. It was because—

Before the thought could fully form, a cry cut through the crowds behind her. A woman split the sea of onlookers and emerged with her arms outstretched. She dropped to the ground beside the boy, sobbing as she leaned toward him.

"My baby . . . my baby . . . Is he okay?"

Skye could see only the back of the woman's head, a bob of big, dark curls that stopped at the woman's shoulders. A silky housecoat with teal and pink flowers draped her slim figure. Something about her screamed affluent and pampered.

Was this the boy's mom? Where had she come from?

Skye glanced behind her. Maybe she'd been at one of the huge mansions on this part of the beach. This stretch of houses was known by locals as Ritzy Row. They were the rental homes that featured ten bedrooms, extravagant pools, and a couple even had lazy rivers.

The rentals cost big bucks.

As in, twelve-thousand-dollars-a-week big bucks.

Skye did a double take when she saw movement across the dunes. A man and a woman rushed over a wooden boardwalk, past a gazebo, and hit the sand. Urgency tinged their steps and movements as they darted toward the scene.

Everything else seemed to fade as Skye watched them.

No, it couldn't be . . .

She swung her gaze back toward the woman leaning over the boy. Then she swerved back toward the couple. Fact collided with emotion in Skye's head until her lungs squeezed.

"Skye?"

She glanced over. Austin lightly touched her arm as he peered at her inquisitively. At some point, he'd pulled a shirt on. Spray from the waves misted his skin.

"Are you okay?" He squinted, still studying her with obvious worry. "You look pale."

She barely heard him. Instead, she turned back to the scene, to where the couple now cut through the crowds, and joined the woman and the boy.

The couple . . . the man with his expensive khaki shorts, boat shoes, and a polo. The woman with blonde hair, set with enough hairspray that it could withstand even this wind, and wearing a dress and pearls.

Pearls . . .

It couldn't be. But it was. That necklace confirmed it.

This couple was Atticus and Ginger Winthrop.

The last time Skye had seen them had been on the worst day of her life.

As the memories rushed back to her, everything blurred around Skye. A part of her life she'd tried to forget roared to the surface, and despair bit as hard and deep as if a shark had clutched her in its teeth and dragged her under.

ALSO BY CHRISTY BARRITT:

BOOKS IN THE LANTERN BEACH UNIVERSE

LANTERN BEACH MYSTERIES

The series that started it all! When a notorious gang puts a bounty on Detective Cady Matthews' head, she has no choice but to hide until she can testify at trial. But her temporary home across the country on a remote North Carolina island isn't as peaceful as she initially thinks. Living under the new identity of Cassidy Livingston, she struggles to keep her investigative skills tucked away. One wrong move could lead to both her discovery and her demise.

#1 Hidden Currents
#2 Flood Watch
#3 Storm Surge
#4 Dangerous Waters
#5 Perilous Riptide
#6 Deadly Undertow

#1 Dark Water
#2 Safe Harbor
#3 Ripple Effect
#4 Rising Tide

LANTERN BEACH GUARDIANS

During a turbulent storm, a child is found on the beach, washed up from the ocean. Making matters worse—the girl can't speak.

#1 Hide and Seek
#2 Shock and Awe
#3 Safe and Sound

LANTERN BEACH BLACKOUT: THE NEW RECRUITS

Four new recruits join Blackout, but someone is determined to teach them a lesson.

#1 Rocco
#2 Axel
#3 Beckett
#4 Gabe

LANTERN BEACH MAYDAY

Kenzie and Jimmy James work on a luxury yacht chartering a dangerous course.

#1 Run Aground
#2 Dead Reckoning
#3 Tipping Point

LANTERN BEACH CHRISTMAS

Catch up with your favorite Lantern Beach characters as they come together to help the town's beloved police chief.

Silent Night

LANTERN BEACH BLACKOUT: DANGER RISING

A new team is formed to combat a new enemy. The mission puts everyone on the line, and failure will mean certain death.

#1 Brandon
#2 Dylan
#3 Maddox
#4 Titus

BEACH BOUND
BOOKS AND BEANS MYSTERIES

When widow Tali Robinson moves to Lantern Beach to renovate an old oceanfront store and turn it into a bookstore/coffee shop, the last thing she expects to find is a human skeleton hidden within the walls. But her troubles don't stop there, and before long she realizes she doesn't have to dig for trouble, she's bound to run into it.

#1 Bound by Murder
#2 Bound by Disaster
#3 Bound by Mystery
#4 Bound by Trouble
#5 Bound by Mayhem

ABOUT THE AUTHOR

USA Today has called Christy Barritt's books "scary, funny, passionate, and quirky."

Christy writes both mystery and romantic suspense novels that are clean with underlying messages of faith. Her books have sold more than four million copies and have won the Daphne du Maurier Award for Excellence in Suspense and Mystery, have been twice nominated for the Romantic Times Reviewers' Choice Award, and have finaled for both a Carol Award and Foreword Magazine's Book of the Year.

She is married to her Prince Charming, a man who thinks she's hilarious—but only when she's not trying to be. Christy is a self-proclaimed klutz, an avid music lover who's known for spontaneously bursting into song, and a road trip aficionado.

When she's not working or spending time with her family, she enjoys singing, playing the guitar, and exploring small, unsuspecting towns where people have no idea how accident-prone she is.

Find Christy online at:

www.christybarritt.com

www.facebook.com/christybarritt

www.twitter.com/cbarritt

Sign up for Christy's newsletter to get information on all of her latest releases here: **www.christybarritt.com/newsletter-sign-up/**

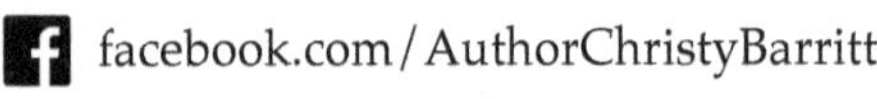 facebook.com/AuthorChristyBarritt

x.com/christybarritt

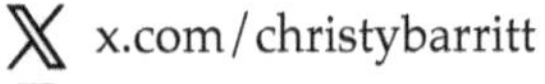 instagram.com/cebarritt